FOUR LADIES

HUSSIN ALKHEDER

Copyright © 2021 Hussin Alkheder.

All rights reserved. No part of this book may be reproduced, stored, or transmitted by any means—whether auditory, graphic, mechanical, or electronic—without written permission of the author, except in the case of brief excerpts used in critical articles and reviews. Unauthorized reproduction of any part of this work is illegal and is punishable by law.

This is a work of fiction. All of the characters, names, incidents, organizations, and dialogue in this novel are either the products of the author's imagination or are used fictitiously.

Because of the dynamic nature of the Internet, any web addresses or links contained in this book may have changed since publication and may no longer be valid.

The cover design by getcover.com
The editing services by William Gould of Eye Edit Books
The interior book format by Miblart.com

*To all the mothers
who lost their lives
due to the
Corona Virus...*

CONTENTS

1

Love in the Time of Corona.... 9
The Green Bus 16
Handmade Crutches 29

2

Hamama................... 38
Lucky Ending............... 43
Baking Bread 50

3

Akev 72
The Power of Words 81
Bedtime Story 88

4

The Writer 98
The Cure................... 107
On the Metro.............. 114

1

An ancient lady, with a big heart,
A mother to many civilizations,
A poem written by the pen of history,
A witness to the journey of humanity,
She is Damascus.

Love in the Time of Corona

I woke up at six thirty, took a shower, and ironed the clothes I was going to wear. The last thing I wanted was for my students to whisper and giggle because their teacher's clothes were not ironed. Then I prepared breakfast for my husband and three children.

I went out on the balcony where my mask hung on the laundry line to dry. Since I can't afford a new mask, I wash the only mask I have, every day after work. My mask is a surgical mask, at least that's what the pharmacist told me, unlike our neighbors who sew masks from old underwear, because they can't afford to buy even one surgical mask. I put on my mask and left the house.

Since I don't have a car, I have to use public transportation, but even if I did have a car, these days, filling the tank would be another luxury I can't afford. I flagged down a small van, and when it stopped beside me, I slid the dirty door open and stepped in. None of the other passengers were wearing masks, only the driver and me.

Above the front passenger seat, a face mask dangled on a thread from the sun visor. No passenger was allowed to sit beside the driver unless they put the face mask on. The driver would refuse to move until they put it on and then remind them to remove it before they stepped down. And yet the passengers in the back were more likely to breathe on him and were much closer.

As the van wove in and out between the other cars, the passengers' bodies swayed with the movements. The whole time their eyes were fixed on my mask with accusatorial looks, as if I was the one breaking the hygienic requirements by wearing it. The sad fact is that most people want to follow the precautions, but they're afraid to act against the herd.

My first period was a writing class, with forty-five high school students packed in the classroom. Only about ten were wearing masks. Today's lecture was titled "Love in the Time of Corona." The students had been asked to present pieces portraying the solidarity of people during these difficult times. They would not be allowed to go up to read the pieces if they weren't wearing a mask.

The first student to go up was Anas, the son of a well-known cardiologist who had passed away recently because of the Corona virus. He searched for his mask and found it in his trouser pocket. It looked as if it had been washed inside the trouser pocket fifty times. It looked funny, all crumpled up on his face.

Anas started, "My father is well known for helping people. He built a charity dispensary to support the poor, who couldn't afford the high cost of an ECG. He dedicated a lot of his time volunteering; going weekly to poor people's homes to examine them and treat them for free. He spent his whole life working to improve his family's image in the eyes of the neighborhood. It shocked us when some ungrateful people paid him back by spreading fake news that he died because of the Corona virus. They tried to ruin his reputation and make us lose face in the community. But their accusations were in vain because many people who were full of love and gratitude toward my father, declared the real reason he died, which was heart failure. They printed posters confirming the truth, and hundreds of our neighbors signed them and posted them along the streets where we live."

While he continued to glorify his father, I was wondering what could be more ruinous to the reputation of a cardiologist than dying of heart failure?

The students applauded enthusiastically for Anas after he finished, as if he'd touched their hearts with his story. I gave the students time to ask questions, then I added a few of my own comments before moving to the second piece.

Next up was Salma, the daughter of an elementary school manager who had died of the virus recently. I had known her father personally. He was a hardworking man. Salma found her mask on the floor beneath her desk. She brushed it off with the back of her hand, put it on, and went to the front of the class.

"My father was a strict principal. His students used to cross to the other side of the road if they saw him approaching on the same pavement they were walking on. The students' families used to call him the Syrian Kim Jong because he didn't allow the students to cut their hair any other way than military style. When he entered a classroom, complete silence must prevail, so when he talked only his voice would be heard. When he spoke, his requests were orders. Not only were his students afraid of him, the teachers were intimidated by his mere presence.

"The amount of love that poured forth from his students after his death was astonishing. I wish he had been alive to witness what the newspapers said about the acts of love from his students after his death, as well as the radio stations, and the TV channels. The solidarity from his students went right across the country. On the day of his burial, the students at his school insisted they wanted to bid him farewell. One of the students was the son of the manager of the fifth district public hospital where his body was. He convinced his father to send my father's body to the school before the burial so the students could say goodbye. It was heartbreaking to see how the students refused to say goodbye without kissing my father's forehead one by one! Of course, they put a mask on my father's face before they started kissing him. I got quite emotional seeing how all of them cried and would not permit the ambulance to leave the school until the end of their school day. It was a real outpouring of love."

Salma went back to her seat, followed by applause even louder than it had been for Anas. I was speechless. The media had criticized the movement of the body, but not the foolhardy actions of the students.

The third student up was Marwa, who is half Lebanese and half Syrian. Her story took place in the village where her mother was from in Lebanon. Marwa is very fashionable. Every day she wears a mask that matches her makeup; today her mask was pink.

"My cousin Badr woke up one day with a fever and cough. My aunt forced him to stay home to recover. But, when rumors spread in the village that Badr had Corona virus, she asked him to go to his work to save the face of the family, in the eyes of the other families in the village. He went out and pretended that everything was okay. However, his red face and labored breathing didn't convince people, and the rumors didn't stop. To prove he was okay, he went all the way into the city to have the nucleic acid test at the hospital.

Two days later, the hospital called to inform them that he had no virus. On the same day, my aunt opened her house and received many of the men and women of the neighborhood to congratulate her for her son's great health. Of course, most of the men brought their Kalashnikovs. The area around my auntie's house looked like a battlefield. They fired round after round into the sky for many long minutes. Everyone wanted to shoot more bullets to prove how much they loved my cousin Badr.

When they entered the house, all the men hugged and kissed him; three kisses on each cheek, as is the custom in Lebanon. It is considered shameful to visit someone without kissing them.

But then the hospital called again to inform them they had made a mistake. They had gotten the paperwork mixed up and the results they'd reported for Badr were for someone else. Badr did in fact have the Corona virus. No one wanted to admit they'd shot so many bullets for nothing, so they all agreed the second call to the house must have been from someone in the village trying to ruin my cousin's reputation."

After Marwa, more students came up and astonished us with similar stories, proof of the amount of love in the people's hearts in this community.

After this class, I had a grade ten grammar class, and then I would normally be done for the day, but, because the geography teacher was under quarantine in his house, I was covering his classes. The social studies teacher had died because of the virus and school management hasn't found a replacement yet, so I have to cover her classes as well. All my teaching days now consist of back-to-back classes. When I finally get home, I am completely drained.

On my way home that evening, I had just stepped down from the van, and was walking the five blocks to my apartment, again avoiding people's eyes, especially those who weren't wearing masks. I was thinking about how the people of Syria were drained after seven years of war. It seems they consider the dangers of the Corona Virus to be minor, in comparison to what they've seen during the years of war. They figure if they could survive the rain of mortar shells over the city and stay alive, how can they be defeated by an unseen virus. The economy was bad, to the point that vendors couldn't stay at home even for one day; they needed to provide for their families. As if the Syrian people didn't face enough calamities during the war, they now have to face the pandemic of Corona.

Last time I was checking the app of Johns Hopkins University, there were over a hundred and twenty-two million cases around the world. Deaths' have exceeded two million and seven hundred thousand globally. When I mention these numbers to any of my colleagues, they tell me that during the war millions of people died in this country.

"Hi, Mona." My neighbor Suzan startled me. I looked up to see her walking towards me.

"Hi Suzan, I'm sorry, my mind was elsewhere."

"I bet you were thinking about what you want to cook for your husband and children.," She laughed, but I merely gave her a weak smile.

"Where is your face mask?" I asked her.

"I just saw Damir over on Thowra street. When I asked him where he was going, he said to the bank, but he didn't have his mask with him. So I gave him my mask to wear so they would allow him to enter the bank."

I was speechless.

"Okay Mona, see you later." She went left, and I went right, continuing toward my building. At that point all I wanted was to wash my mask and be alone.

The Green Bus

Eight years have passed since the war ignited in Syria. It was as if a tornado had swept through the country, leaving damaged cities, a deficit economy, and broken humans. When I visited my family in 2019, the war had subsided in the cities and moved to the eastern and northern borders. There were no flights allowed to land at Damascus International Airport because of the sanctions imposed on us. I had to land in Beirut and travel by car to Damascus. The trip from Beirut airport to Damascus city took half a day at least, which before the war used to take only two hours. The delay was because of the Lebanese immigration in the airport and the plethora of security points along the way to Damascus.

After we crossed the Syrian border, there were no indications of the distraction of war, except the security points; the driver must stop at each point and present each of the passenger's passports. When we reached the outskirts of Damascus, the heavy smell of sorrow hung in the air. The city was totally different from how it had been during my last visit, nine years earlier. Random buildings had either been knocked down or burned down from the rain of mortar shells that fell on the city in the last few years. Security inspections on every street hindered traffic to the point of exasperation. The variety of vehicles in the street consisted of a collection of ancient, tired looking cars, hardly a spot intact on their dirty bodies. There was no trace of expensive luxury cars in the streets, either they'd been stolen and used as booby traps or their owners didn't dare drive them. An expensive car was the easiest way for criminals to identify a kidnap target in those days, and they would often hold a family member for ransom. To me, Damascus city was like a gorgeous lady who had been put under a spell of infinite beauty, despite her ten-thousand-year age. However, the pain of the last few years broke the spell and exposed the crumbling, dusty face of a beldame.

When we arrived at the place where I live, the street was deserted. None of the screams or cheering from kids that used to play outside all day long. The trees were dead or dying; the asphalt marked with shallow flower shaped holes, the result of falling mortar shells. Many of the buildings had holes in their walls for the same reason. The few people on the street stopped what they were doing and stared at me with bowed shoulders.

Of course, my family was happy to see me after so many years away. They had aged not only in years, but the burdens of the war had taken their toll as well. They told a lot of stories that would make a child's hair turn white. Before the war, I would never have thought these horrible things could happen in Syria in a thousand years. They showed me the hole in the balcony wall where a mortar shell hit. Thankfully, no one was at home at the time. The economic situation had returned to that of the eighties, when people waited in long lines for hours to get the basic food items like rice, sugar, and cooking oil. My sisters told me how getting a gas cylinder nowadays was nearly impossible, and most of the citizens now cook on electric stoves. However, they're forced to wait for the few hours per day when electricity would be available. Most of the day there was none. The value of the currency went down ten times, while prices of fruit and vegetables jumped through the roof, and salaries didn't increase proportionally.

Next morning, I left the house to renew my passport. I could easily have taken a taxi, despite the fact that taxi drivers had stopped using their meters and were asking whatever price they wanted. They justified it because of the decrease in the value of the currency. However, I had always used public transport before leaving my country, and enjoyed people's company, so I decided to do the same this time.

The number of buses was noticeably less than I remembered, and whenever a bus did come, it was always overflowing with people. So, having waited a considerable time, I was forced to squeeze in among the standing room only, shoulder to shoulder passengers. The odor of bodies was enough to make the head swim. Around me the crowd of men and women, poorly dressed, tales of hardship imprinted on their faces, their hunger and need showed plainly in their eyes. I was relieved when I finally stepped down from the bus.

I found the passport office on the second floor of the immigration building, empty except for the staff, unlike the old days. Everyone who could leave the country during the war had left already. Millions of Syrians fled to Europe, and you can find Syrian refugees in most countries, even Sudan and Egypt.

After finishing my business at the passport office, I spent hours walking the streets, with tears in my eyes and sorrow in my heart over the condition of the city. When I reached home on foot, I was even more exhausted emotionally than physically.

Back when I was still living in my country, I used to overcome distress by writing about whatever was overwhelming my brain. It was an effective method to release my tension and anxiety. But, if I wasn't in the mood to write, I'd read things I had written on previous occasions. I decided I wanted to read some of my own writing from before I left Syria. Back then, everything was great. The economy was growing rapidly, and people from different religions and sects lived together in harmony and synergy.

I headed to the room that used to be mine before I left the country. Just a simple room, with a single bed, a closet, a desk and the library, which was a small wooden cupboard in the corner, right next to the desk with a small lamp on it. The library was filled with non-fiction books, novels, magazines, and personal diaries. Glancing proudly over my treasures, I took down the pile of diaries, threw them on the bed, sat down next to them, and looked for a story similar to what happened to me today but from years before the war. I selected the diary from 2009 and started reading. In a short time, I had another big lump in my throat.

* * *

The cool breeze on my face felt like silky feathers, which only added to my joy and delight. Pulses of enthusiasm and optimism beat inside me. I'm not sure if it was because of the breeze on my skin or the rain of prayers my mom showered over me before I left home.

Bin Assaker Street, where I live, is one of Damascus's busiest streets. While I waited for transportation, plenty of vehicles passed, but the best of them were the new green buses which were able to accommodate a lot of passengers. I enjoy the company of people while they're carrying out their daily errands.

I raised my arm when I noticed a bus approaching. As usual, it stopped ten meters past me, so I had to run and jump aboard before the driver stomped the fuel pedal and the bus sped off with a roar. I paid the driver ten Syrian pounds. He took the money and gave me the ticket while driving, without even looking at me.

The bright yellow seats faced each other in sets of four. At the back, the seats were higher than the ones in the front, and in the middle was a clear space for passengers to stand. I went all the way to the back and sat. From there, I would have a very good view during my journey.

The bus was not full, passengers were sitting randomly here and there. We swayed with the jerky movements of the bus, both from the stop and go in the traffic jam, and when stopping to pick up and drop off passengers. Drivers are only required to stop at the bus stops, but they tend to stop wherever a passenger waves them down.

If I were to watch the bus pass while standing on the street, I would only see people sitting there with no expectations, except arriving at their destination. From inside the bus, however, it is a different story. I could notice odd behavior or mannerisms without being able to guess their reason.

Two seats away from me sat a middle-aged mother with her baby girl in her arms. The mother wore a dark blue lint-covered coat, shiny from ironing, and a pale blue scarf covering her head. The baby girl was very cute and hyperactive, dressed in fine new clothes. Clearly,

1: *The Green Bus*

the mother deprived herself throughout the year, so she could afford expensive clothes for her child. The woman's affection was obvious when she gazed at her baby girl, clutching her firmly whenever the bus swayed or bumped. Her love was beautiful to behold.

In the next seat there was a teenager wearing a rather conservative light gray coat covering her modestly, and a scarf hiding her hair. She focused straight ahead, avoiding meeting the eyes of the young man sitting opposite. He was extremely handsome, with caramel hair and honey eyes. He wore a light t-shirt which did little to hide his masculine chest and tanned arms.

Beside him was an old woman wearing shabby multicolored clothes, much too heavy for the weather. Her yellowish white hair seemed to be covered with an oily substance that caused it to dangle wetly on her neck. Her face was full of deep wrinkles, evidence of the tragedies she has been exposed to during her lifetime. Her eyes were pure light blue and often caused fear in those who saw them. Her lips trembled like she might start to cry at any moment. Her eyes darted left and right without focusing on anything. She looked as though she was carrying the sorrow of the seven continents on her soul.

Few of the other passengers were unremarkable, not because they weren't important, but because they were too plain to be noticed. The driver stopped and picked up two fashionable looking young women. Tall and thin, they wore brand name clothes, shoes, and bags. Their fingers were ornamented with gemstone rings, their nails perfectly polished, and large elaborate earrings dangling from their ears. Their necklines revealed tanned skin. There were still plenty of unoccupied seats, but they preferred to stand. As they glanced around at the other passengers, they whispered to each other and giggled like teenagers, especially after looking at any young man, whether standing or sitting. Most of the young men smiled when the girl's eyes met theirs.

An old man limped onto the bus, leaning on a walking stick. Dressed in worn-out clothes, this old man looked like a beggar. Though in Syria, we don't call the beggars homeless, because no one sleeps in the street. Even though they are poor, they have a place to sleep, a room, an attic, or even a roof. Despite plenty of other free seats, he went and sat next to the mother still clutching her baby girl. He smiled at the child and when she returned his smile, he touched her tiny hand with a finger and made funny noises to make her laugh. The result was not only the baby laughing, but a few of the people around him as well. He was so funny. The mother remained stiff as a post and as pale as an eggshell. The old man took a coin from his pocket, the silver shining brightly between his dirty thumb and finger. The mother put her hand up to prevent the baby from taking the money. The old man tried to convince the mother to accept the coin and give it to the baby, but the mother kept refusing.

Three boys boarded, their childish voices much too loud, as if they were the only ones on the bus. Two of them sat next to each other, while the third sat facing them. One of the boys in the back seat took money from his pocket and threw it at the third boy as if he was throwing a stick and asking his dog to go fetch it, and said, "Go and pay the driver."

"Do you think I am your family servant? Go and pay him yourself."

"Why are you acting like a baby, what's wrong with moving your fat ass to pay the driver our fees?" The one who threw the money said.

The boy took the money reluctantly. Huffing and puffing, he headed to the front to pay. As soon as he got up, a man sat in his empty seat. When the boy came back and saw that his seat had been taken, he threw the tickets at his friends, gave them a toxic scowl, and said in a nasty voice, "Are you happy now? I don't have a place to sit." His two friends burst out laughing loudly at him. The woman sitting across the aisle smiled at the angry boy, stood up and asked him to come and take her seat. The three boys yelled, begging her to sit back in her seat, thanking her. "We can fit the three of us on these two seats," the ringleader told her. The passengers were smiling. I think they admired the generosity of the woman and the reaction of the boys.

As the swaying bus proceeded, passengers continued to get on and off. Hundreds of cars passed all around us, producing huge amounts of carbon dioxide in addition to the noise pollution. The taxi drivers in this city honk their horns incessantly, usually for no apparent reason, as if they're performing in a circus.

A middle-aged man in untidy clothes was standing next to the teenage girl in the conservative coat and headscarf. He pushed his crotch forward until it touched her shoulder, so that every movement the bus made, he was pressing his private parts against her. It was disgusting how he took advantage of the number of passengers crowded on the bus. The teenager was red in the face, her eyes fixed on the floor. I thought if she didn't ask him to move away, no one would help her. Surprisingly, the young man with the muscles stood up and asked the girl politely if she would exchange seats with him, which she did gladly, and thanked him in a low voice. The young man sat down and glared at the standing man, who suddenly seemed as if he wanted the earth to swallow him at that moment.

All the empty seats were taken and among the many passengers were few women standing. As a rule, the males would give up their seats for the females. One man was sitting three seats away from where the two fashionable young women were standing, still whispering and giggling. He raised his hand to attract their attention and pointed to them to come and take his seat. It was very rude of him, because between him and the two young women there were at least four older standing women. Of course they weren't as fashionable or as attractive as the two young, tanned women. The two young women ignored him and giggled, then turned and faced the other way to avoid looking at him.

The old lady with the oily yellow-white hair asked in a loud voice for the driver to drop her in front of the Public Police Park. All the passengers, including me, were surprised, as this particular bus doesn't go past the Public Police Park. The old lady yelled once more when she didn't receive any response from the driver and the bus wasn't slowing down.

"We don't pass near the Public Police Park," the driver said finally without taking his eyes off the road.

"I always ride this bus and go to the Police Park, and now you are telling me you don't pass the park? Why don't you just say, you don't want to drop me?" she yelled.

A few passengers turned their heads to hide their smiles. The driver kept swearing that this line doesn't pass the Police Park.

"I am a cow to ride with you," the old woman shouted at the driver, "It is a conspiracy against me,

I am an old woman and my knees are hurting me, how will I reach the park now?"

"I swear by the bones of all the prophets..." the driver was screaming when she interrupted him.

"Stop here and let me down, I will walk, even though my feet hurt." The bus stopped, and she descended, repeating at the top of voice, "I am an old woman and my knees are hurting..." Her voice was audible even as the bus moved away, she was screaming so loudly.

The bus drove on steadily for a while with no stops. By then we were on Adawi Highway, and the noise of the traffic drowned out the voices of the passengers. When the old man sitting next to the mother and her baby girl asked the driver to stop, the driver didn't hear. The old man asked again, but the driver still didn't hear him. The old man started to shout, "Abu Khara (the father of shit), TizYallali (insulting mimic), Abu Khara, TizYallali, drop me down here." He appealed to the people standing around him and said, "Look everyone, look at Abu Khara, he must be deaf." A few people yelled at the driver, asking him to stop. The bus finally stopped, but unfortunately, it was a long way past the spot where he'd wanted to get down at. He exited, cursing and insulting the driver as he went. The driver merely smiled and didn't respond.

The bus continued on and a few moments later we reached the spot where I wanted to get off. I approached the front and merely glanced at the driver. He immediately understood that I wanted to get down. He stopped, and I descended, still filled with happiness.

* * *

I shut the notebook still in my hand, staring at the wall. My mom entered the room, and I smiled at her, but she didn't smile back. With a serious face, she sat down on the foot of the bed and asked, "What is the matter?"

I told her what had happened earlier and what I had just read from the notebook.

"You scared me to death, I thought something terrible had happened to you." She stood up and beckoned, "Come with me."

I followed her out onto the balcony. We were on the ninth floor, overlooking the ancient city wall which encircled hundreds of Damascus's legendary older houses, each with a fountain in the center of the yard, surrounded by citrus aurantium trees, which cast their shade over anyone sitting around the fountains enjoying a cup of Arabic coffee. All the houses are of similar height, with the only one taller being the lofty Umayyad Grand Mosque, with its three high minarets and the dome in the center of the roof, looking much like a castle. I used to sit on this balcony to watch the sunset, smoke a hookah, and drink tea. It was my daily ritual back then.

"What do you see," she asked, pointing towards the old city.

"Hundreds of old houses," I answered, "of the legendary old Damascus. Right?"

"Yes, that's true, it is the legendary old Damascus, but how did it become legendary? Was it because of all the stones, or might it have been the people who built the houses with those stones?"

"Damascus is one of the oldest continuously inhabited cities on earth," I said, looking out across the old city. "I guess it's the people who are responsible for that, not the buildings."

"Anyone can read the history of the countless hard times the people of this city went through. Hard times, like the past few years of war. And yet the people are still here."

"But Mom, earlier today on the bus, I didn't get the feeling that the people are still alive. It felt like those people were just bodies with no souls."

"What you saw today proves my point. During the war, hundreds of towns and villages were destroyed and their inhabitants fled to Damascus. Before the war Damascus had three million occupants, but after the war there were eight million. The people you saw today are the very people who fled to the city and were welcomed by the ones you saw nine years ago, as you mentioned in your story. The ones who are full of life are still here, but they're spread out among the others who came from elsewhere."

"Oh mom, how can you be so positive after seeing what's happened to this country?"

"It's not what we see that creates our perception, it's how we see things," she said. "During the rain of mortar shells on this city, a family died while having breakfast in one of old Damascus's famous restaurants when a mortar hit it."

"Oh god. Why did they go to the restaurant under such conditions?"

"It shows that the people of this city refuse to stop living despite the danger. It shows that the people are full of the joy of living. There have been many other cases like that one. There was a group of women who died while having their weekly breakfast gathering when a mortar hit the house of their host."

"I am more certain than ever this city will stay alive as long as it has ladies like you in it."

"Thank you. I think of this city as a grand lady who has created generations of legendary ladies," she said with a satisfied smile.

Handmade Crutches

Hadiya took one look at the blood flowing from her left hand, and her heartbeat accelerated. She bit her lip, shut her eyes, and pulled the jagged tip of the large splintered piece of wood from her hand. She didn't want to cry or scream in front of her four daughters or her son Khaled, especially when they were already yelling and pacing the floor erratically as soon as they saw the blood.

"Calm down, it's nothing serious," Hadiya said.

"Mama, what are you talking about? Look at the puddle of blood on the floor," Zakiya, the youngest daughter said, with tears streaming down her cheeks.

Hadiya forced a smile, "Get me a towel, please." Zakiya jumped up as if she'd been stung by a hornet and came back with an old worn-out towel. Worn towels were all they had because it was all they could afford.

Farah, Marwa, and Ro'wa gathered around their mother like bees swarming around their queen. They wrapped her hand in the towel as tightly as they could, but the wound was deep, and the towel was quickly soaked in blood.

Farah looked at Khaled, and screamed at him through her tears, "It's all your fault. If Mama was not making new crutches for you, she wouldn't have cut her hand like this."

Hadiya felt a lump rise in her throat. Choking back a cry, she said, "No, Darling. It is not Khaled's fault. Please don't blame him for something he didn't do. I should not have tried to use the butcher knife, but I don't have a saw." She glanced at Khaled apologetically. Her son was fourteen years old and shorter than all his peers, because he had been born with a congenital bone disorder. The tension of his muscles put stress on his soft bones, resulting in bowed arms and legs. He was not able to get around without crutches since he couldn't bend his knees. He had a very large head, relative to his small body, and a triangular shaped face because of overdevelopment of his cranial bones and underdevelopment of the bones in his face.

His shoulders were prominent because the old crutches he had been using were too long for him. They were handmade and of different lengths, which caused his left shoulder to be higher than the right one. However, after the crutches mysteriously fell from the third-floor balcony and were reduced to splinters, Hadiya thought if she could buy proper crutches, it would be healthier for him. Unfortunately, there was not enough money for such things.

"Look at all this blood," Farah said, still sobbing.

Marwa looked at Farah and said, "This morning, I went with Mama, to our grandfather's shop to ask for money to buy new crutches. But he said our father hasn't sent him any money for a long time."

"We must be patient with your father. He went to Dubai to earn money to pay off his debts. Soon he will come back to live with us again," Hadiya said, reminding herself, as well as her daughters, of the reason she was making the crutches.

"Why did grandfather not just give us money?" Ro'wa asked. "He is a successful merchant and always brags in front of everyone that he is the Godfather of the merchants?" She was holding her mom's wounded hand gently with both hands, as if she was cradling a newly born bird.

"That poor old man, has three families to feed," Hadiya said, doing a poor job of convincing herself that her father-in-law was not able to help his indebted son because of his three wives; each one living in a big house.

"You must go to the hospital Mama, your hand needs stitches," Farah said, wiping her moist eyes with her sleeve.

"Ok, let me finish these crutches, and my hero, Khaled, will accompany me." Hadiya smiled at Khaled. It was out of the question for her to leave the apartment without a man to accompany her.

With the help of her four daughters, Hadiya finished making the crutches, then helped Khaled to stand up and tuck them under his arms. She didn't see a smile on his face. *But that's ok*, she thought. *Who would be happy getting handmade crutches instead of professionally made ones?*

Getting dressed would only take her a few minutes. She put on the only coat she owned, which was old and shiny from the years of washing and ironing. She covered her hair with a fading black scarf, slightly older than the coat, slipped her feet into her only pair of shoes, and she was ready. The process of dressing Khaled usually took over thirty minutes, but fortunately she had dressed him that morning soon after he woke up. Dressing him with only one good hand would have been challenging. She wouldn't allow her daughters to help their brother to dress and undress, it wouldn't be proper. Khaled had a severe case of hammertoe due to wearing shoes that were too small all the time. The rotten smell of his feet was unbearable no matter how long he soaked them. Her neighbor Um-Fathi advised her to put salt with the water to help reduce the smell, but unfortunately, Hadiyah couldn't afford to buy extra salt. She didn't mind the smell so much. He is, after all, her beloved son.

Her daughters helped her remove the blood-soaked towel and wrap her hand with a clean one, which became stained with blood immediately. She refused to let any of them accompany her and Khaled because she didn't want them to interrupt their studies.

Taking a taxi was out of the question. She could not afford such luxury. Riding the public bus would be torture, but she didn't have a choice. Khaled would never be able to hobble the 5 km to the hospital. She thought how lucky she was because the public hospitals in Syria are free. She thanked God for this blessing.

The knocking of the new handmade crutches seemed louder than usual as she and Khaled descended the steps and stepped out on the street. But of course, they would be louder; the wood of the crutches had not softened from use yet, like the old ones. For a fraction of a second, she wondered if Khaled was angry with her. But no, she erased that sinful thought from her mind immediately. She had brought up her children based on the precepts of unconditional love and forgiveness. He wouldn't do that.

Hadiya and Khaled reached the bus stop. Actually, just a spot where people usually stand to wait for buses since the buses would stop wherever and whenever a passenger waved them down. A crowd of people, mostly men, were standing there ready to jump aboard a still moving bus as it passed, because the buses never stop completely. The drivers tap the brakes but keep moving forward at a lower speed to allow passengers either to jump from the street onto the bus or from the bus to the street. For most of the waiting people, that was ok, but for Hadiya and Khaled, this was extremely challenging. Many buses came by, but each time she wasn't able to jump and pull Khaled with her. The buses slowed several meters ahead of where they stood, but each time Khaled couldn't hobble fast enough. Finally, a bus slowed directly in front of them, and with a rapidly beating heart she grabbed Khaled's hand and they both jumped for the bus's open-door frame. To Hadiya's embarrassment, they ended up sprawled on the filthy floor of the bus. A couple of men offered her helping hands, but she just thanked them and pulled herself up. She was not allowed to touch strange men, but she was happy to see them helping Khaled back to his feet.

Her left hand was bleeding more now, along with an added burning sensation. The bus was crowded, and all the people stared at them wide-eyed, especially at Khaled. To prevent him from seeing the scared looks in the people's eyes, she kept looking at her beloved Khaled with eyes full of affection and a sweet smile. His ruddy complexion shone like a flame out of sensitivity. The parts of his eyes that would normally be white were blue due to his medical condition. This caused people to stare and shiver. But Hadiya loved him and saw him as a most handsome son.

When the bus driver got a look at Hadiya's bloody hand, he brought the bus to a complete stop in front of the City Hospital out of sympathy. Khaled was able to get down on his own and save them from the embarrassment of flopping on the ground again. She was so grateful for this driver; she looked up at the sky and prayed for him to get whatever he desired.

As they went in through the emergency gate, they found the place teeming with scores of people just like them. People stared at Khaled less now though, since everyone there had their own personal calamities to distract them from the problems of others. Hadiya and Khaled spent a few hours waiting for their turn. The doctor who finally attended them was very young, barely graduated, or maybe he was still a medical student. It didn't matter; he was like a healing balm with his friendly smile, positive attitude, and sweet words. She forgot about the pain in her hand, and the suffering of waiting so long in this dingy place. Her hand was stitched up, and they began their journey back home.

This time, she asked Khaled to grasp her left arm firmly above the elbow as she intended to use her right hand to grab hold of something when she jumped on the bus so she would be able to pull Khaled along with her.

A few buses passed before she was able to jump aboard one. She grabbed the metal bar near the door and pulled Khaled with all her strength. The bus driver realized the difficulty of their mission too late, and when he pressed the brakes to stop, she and Khaled crashed into the front transom, and one of the crutches shattered under the weight of Khaled's body. A few passengers stopped to help her and Khaled to their feet.

She looked at Khaled and smiled. "Don't worry, I will make a new one for you as soon as we reach home. For now, we have the other crutch, it will be enough if you hold on to my arm." Khaled didn't say anything. She wished she understood the emotions raging in his head, since his eyes showed no positive feelings. All the way back to their apartment, she avoided the stares of people by keeping her smile focused on Khaled. She couldn't understand why he continued to avoid eye contact. *Maybe he's embarrassed by my old clothes*, she thought.

She couldn't take the shattered crutch with her when they got off the bus, as she had only one good hand and she needed that to help Khaled hobble home. This time the driver stopped the bus completely and allowed them to get down safely, for which she was very grateful.

Their home was four blocks away from the main road and on the journey back, her arm hurt from where Khaled was holding on. His grip was so tight and strong, which caused her enormous pain, her arm almost pierced by his nails. She didn't know why he was using all of his strength. *Is he afraid to fall, or is he afraid I'll hurry home and leave him?* His hobbling was so slow.

That's when she heard Khaled sobbing. Stopping in her tracks, she bent down so her face was level with his. He was crying as if he was carrying the sorrow of the world on his shoulders. Cheeks wet with tears, he looked at her sorrowfully. She hugged him tightly, then unable to hold back her own tears, she too started to cry; the shoulder of his shirt soon became wet from her tears.

"I didn't mean to put you through all of this suffering," Khaled's words, heavy with sorrow and pain, burst from his lips between gasping sobs, "Mama, why? Why are you so good to everyone, even the people who are not good to you? I love you so much Mama and I want to protect you. I want to hold you in my heart, keep you safe from all the cruelties of life."

His words made Hadiya's day, and she promptly forgot all about her pain.

Their sobbing drew stares from many passersby, but she didn't care.

Hadiya mysteriously passed away a few years later. The details are in the murder mystery novel The Daughter of Patience.

2

A young lady, with a gorgeous shape,
A mother to many ambitious humans,
An illustration of perfection,
A comfortable cradle for the wealthiest,
She is Dubai.

Hamama

Back in 2008, Dubai's roads had been upside down ever since RTA started the construction of Metro Dubai. Many of the private educational institutions had been moved from the inner city to Dubai's Academic City along al-Ain Fast Highway. I was working full time, I could only attend evening classes, and by that time of day, the roads of the academic city are deserted because most educational institutions are closed for the day.

One evening, on my way to class, I noticed a dark spot on the asphalt ahead, so I reduced my speed to try to figure out what it was. It was a pitiful scene. A gray pigeon (Hamama), with half of its body crushed flat and the other half intact, the blood soaking the feathers had turned the gray to black. I drove carefully around the dead bird, then accelerated so as not to be late for my class. The vision of the pitiful scene was still in my mind when I reached the classroom.

As it turned out, the teacher had not yet arrived. The class consisted of twelve students from different countries, most of whom had come to Dubai for work. All of them were paying huge sums of money to improve their English in this costly city. Better English would allow them to get better jobs, as well as being able to blend in with the general population of the city.

2: Hamama

I found them immersed in a heated discussion. It soon became clear that emotions were high. I didn't want to interrupt them, so I just listened.

"They have no sensitivity. They're even willing to drive over a donkey, not only a bird or cat." Khaled is from Egypt and often disagrees with the opinions of the Emiratis.

"Anyone who could do such a thing hasn't even a tiny bit of mercy. Someone gets in their way and they just knock him down and drive over him, just like they did to that helpless bird." Kasandra, a woman in her forty's, waved her arms and made motions as she spoke, imitating driving a car over something. She's from Colombia and has finished all the levels in the institute and then repeated them all over again. When I asked her why she would do that the first time we met, she changed the topic. I didn't insist on an answer then because I felt she didn't really have a reason, unless she just wanted to meet hot guys like me. I'm only kidding.

Maximillian said, "I can't picture that crime in my head, I stopped my bright yellow Bentley on the shoulder of the road." Everyone in the class knows he drives an old Kia he bought second hand with over a hundred thousand kilometers on the odometer.

"Then I started to calculate the speed that monster must have been driving for that poor bird not to be able to fly out of the way. Imagine with me my friends, maybe he was driving 200 km/h or even 240. I couldn't bear to look at the sad sight as tears fell from my eyes. I got back in my Bentley and stomped on the gasoline pedal. The tires squealed terribly like a scared woman, I'm sure it almost caused the bird's soul to jump back into its body. I think I need to change the tires also, oof." Maximillian possesses an unbridled imagination, and most of the time he won't stop talking, until someone interrupts him.

Fairuz said, "What weird times. People killing vulnerable creatures that might have a family somewhere. Who will feed this poor bird's offspring? I can't bear the thought that those fluffy little chicks will go to sleep hungry." Fairuz is Turkish; a housewife trying to improve her English so she can keep up with her children, who were already talking more fluently in English than their mother tongue. It's much the same for most of the foreign students in Dubai.

"What a despicable troll. If he was in front of me right now, I would beat him soundly. It must have been someone who doesn't care about destroying an innocent animal." Erikal is a fit young woman from Latvia. Her pretty face was red at that moment; her words dripping with rage.

Shahzad said, "I believe we must impose extreme sanctions on the driver of that vehicle, because of the non-compliance with the laws that every citizen must follow. Such a driver exposes himself and those around him to unnecessary danger, which is often the reason for traffic accidents."

His wife, Sarafet, interrupted her husband as usual. She had to head him off before he took advantage of being in a classroom, and start lecturing the group, as if we were members of parliament. "Possibly this poor driver is dead by now, because of your curses."

Shahzad frowned at his wife, and snapped at her, "You call this monster a poor driver?" He shook his head. "If I live a thousand years, I won't understand you women."

"Of course, you will never understand us," Sarafet said with a twisted mouth, "Because you're dumb."

2: Hamama

"Yes, I must be dumb to marry a woman like you." His face was red now too, and a vein stood out on his forehead.

Sarafet jumped up, toppling her chair over, and making a racket. She snatched up her handbag and left the classroom. No one intervened. It wasn't the first time Sarafet had left the classroom after an argument with Shahzad.

Hamid said, "That driver is a loser. He doesn't have the skills or experience to drive 180 km/h, while answering his Blackberry messenger with one hand, holding a lit cigar in the other, and steering with his knees." The young man from Dubai was obsessed with the world of cars and races. He always wore an original Ferrari jacket.

I started to say, "We don't know what…" when, Arlina, our teacher, entered the classroom, and all of us stood up out of respect. No one was interested in what I had to say any more.

"I apologize for the delay. I had a small problem on the drive here…"

Hamid interrupted her, "Teacher, do you need to borrow my car?"

"Oh, that's so sweet. Thank you, but…" Arlina paused and stared at the back of the classroom. We all turned our heads to see Maya hiding her face in her crossed arms, hunched over her desk, sobbing silently. Arlina approached Maya with honest concern on her face and asked, "What's wrong, Maya? Are you ok?"

"Should we call an ambulance?" Shahzad asked.

A few students rolled their eyes at that.

Maya was the youngest, a girl from Sweden. We all respected her politeness and liked her blithe spirit. She was the perfect example of a happy person, and a fine example of a positive human being.

Arlina reached Maya's desk and put a hand on her shoulder, "What's wrong sweetie?"

We all gathered around the teacher, and Maya, who was trying very hard to suppress her sobs. After our repeated questions and the teacher expressing her concerns, Maya finally raised her head. Her face was red, and her eyes swollen from crying. She tried to speak but only managed to gasp and sniff loudly every few words. Gradually, each of us began to understand, and we all stood there like statues. The shock on our faces, and the guilt filling our hearts, was due to our immature and unfair judgment.

Only Arlina was mystified by our guilty faces.

Lucky Ending

I was driving my Toyota Corolla to Dubai International Airport to drop Mullah Abdullah al-Allab to catch his flight back to Damascus. Mullah Abdullah is a neighbor of ours back in Damascus. He had been in Dubai for a few days to attend an Islamic convention. A few days earlier my father had called and informed me I must stick to the Mullah like his shadow and fulfill all his needs during his stay in Dubai.

It wasn't hard for me, as a sales executive, to manage my clients' visits during the time the Mullah was occupied, so I could be at his side whenever he was free. After all, it was only for five days. The Mullah was known as a hero by everyone in my neighborhood in Damascus, because in 2010 before the war started, he uncovered a dangerous extremist organization, and opened the government's eyes to the plans of such groups who were mostly financed and controlled from beyond our borders.

During those five days, I had asked the Mullah all kinds of questions about how he got through it? Why he did it since he was a religious person and not a police officer? Was it true that the extremists group kidnapped him? Was it true that he uncovered the murderer of our neighbor Hadiyah? and many more questions.

I came to the conclusion that he was just a normal human being like everyone else. In my opinion, he was a little weird for three reasons: first, a religious person nowadays didn't call himself Mullah anymore; second, he wears a red fez instead of a turban which was a hundred-year-old tradition; and third, he keeps saying he's a detective.

He was staying in Oriental Palace, a five-star hotel along the beach at Jumeirah. When I picked him up from the hotel, he was wearing his ordinary religious garb, a cream dish-dash, a coffee-colored cloak and of course his exotic red velvet fez. I put all his luggage in the trunk, except he held onto a black, fake leather handbag. He removed his red fez when he got into the passenger seat and set it on his lap, since it was too tall to be worn inside the car. He put his handbag on the floor between his feet.

Steeped in silence, we stopped at a red traffic light near Madinat Jumeirah, opposite Burj al-Arab. I glanced over at him and smiled as I waited for the light to change. He was in his fifties, the same age as my father, but he has the wrinkled skin of a hundred-year-old man, and his eyes spoke of deep underlying pain. God only knows what atrocities he's seen.

When we reached Sheikh Zaid Road, I noticed how he was stretching his neck to get a better look at the legendary towers. I knew it wasn't his first time in Dubai, but I didn't blame him. I've been in Dubai for a number of years now, and every time I pass along this street I'm still enchanted by those towers. He asked without tearing his eyes away from the towers, "These towers look perfect from outside, do you think they are also perfect on the inside?"

"They are wonderful and elegant and no doubt perfect inside and outside. They were built by an international construction companies which always finish their projects on time," I said as we crossed the Aal Maktoum bridge toward Deira.

"So not like back home, stuck together with spit and promise?" he said, laughing at his own joke. I forced out a small fake laugh and said, "Here, the work has to meet international standards, otherwise those towers wouldn't be so perfect."

"I registered with an association for a new house thirty years ago in the area of Kuswa in the Damascus suburbs." He sighed.

"What do you mean by association?" I asked, as I wondered to myself, where Dubai will be in thirty years.

"It's a construction company that sells houses on monthly payments. They start building from the money they collect every month. Whoever pays quickest is at the top of the list to receive their house."

"Thirty years is a long time. Were you paying only a hundred dollars a month?" He didn't seem to find my sarcasm funny.

"I waited thirty years, and received my house a year before the war," he said, "but without ceramic. I didn't want the ceramic the association provided, because it was cheap and low quality. I ordered Italian ceramic."

I thought, *where did he get the money to order Italian ceramic*, but asked instead, "Did you buy the ceramic online?"

He looked at me as if I was talking Turkish and asked, "What online? The ceramic supply stores in our city have Italian brands."

"The Italian ceramic was not the problem," he continued shaking his head sarcastically. "The problem was, after we installed the ceramic, I opened the faucet in the bathroom, and no water came out, just a gurgling noise. *Strange, a faucet without water*. I tried other faucets, in the toilet, and in the kitchen. No water. Not a drop of water from any faucet in the house. I went down to the basement, to check the water meter, but it seemed fine, no apparent damage. The next day I started a series of hand kissing to convince the plumber of the association to come and check the pipes. Who knew convincing him to come to the house would take almost a month? One week he was sick, one week he had a mourning ceremony, one week he had to attend his granddaughter's birthday party. After a very long wait, he finally came. When he entered the kitchen, he took one glance and said, 'We need to break all the ceramic to find the problem!!"

"I yelled, 'are you serious?'" the Mullah was silent for a while, as if he was remembering his struggle with that plumber, "The plumber answered, 'It's the only way. We have to break all the ceramic to find out where the damage is so we can repair it.'"

I laughed when I heard the Mullah mimicking the voice of the plumber.

The Mullah continued, 'And you want to change the pipes?' I asked the plumber, and he answered, 'Yes, of course, when we break the ceramic the pipes will be damaged also, so you will need new pipes.'"

"So, how will you know where the problem is if you damage the pipes during the breaking of the ceramic?' I asked."

"The plumber answered, 'that is my job, and that's what I need to do, take it or leave it.'"

The Mullah looked across at me as he spoke, but I kept my eyes on the road most of the time, taking short glances at him from time to time.

"Of course, they broke the ceramic and changed the pipes. The plumber informed me the reason for the problem was a mistake in the design. After they finished, I headed to the first faucet I saw and turned it on. I was happy to see the water flowing, even though it was kind of yellowish. At least it was water. You know, a house without water is worthless."

"Of course, you were relieved, even though you lost the cost of the Italian ceramic," I said and slowed to a stop at the Qosais-Sharjah traffic light.

"Oh, I wish," the Mullah said sarcastically. "I'll tell you what happened."

"I decided to test the heating system." He gestured with his right hand in the air as if he was turning a small dial. "I turned on the central heater which distributes the hot water to the radiators, and every few minutes I touched the radiator in the hallway, but no heat. I thought, *maybe the heating capacity is low, and I need to wait longer*. I waited one hour, two hours, three hours, no heat. I ran from room to room, radiator to radiator. I just wanted to know where the problem was. But no clue."

The light turned green, and I drove on.

"Of course, a new series of hand kissing started with an assistant of the engineer of the association," the Mullah continued. "One day he was sick, one day he was busy, one day he had a marriage anniversary, one day he was invited to his aunt's house, one day his car was not working, and after a whole month, his highness came to the house. After less than one minute's observation he said, 'we must break down the walls and change the hot-water pipes.' So they broke my house walls and changed all the hot-water pipes. Thank God the heating system in my house was working again."

"Thank God. Now you are living in the house, all happy and comfortable?"

"Huh, you'll never guess what happened next," he said with a half groan, half sigh.

"What more could happen after smashing the ceramic and breaking down the walls? Don't tell me they demolished the house and rebuilt it."

He said, "The doors in the house are made from beechwood, a most desirable wood for doors and furniture, but very expensive. The doors were imported, and hand engraved with enchanting flowers and trees. They cost me a fortune to have them installed in the house.

"A few days later, after the problem of the heaters was solved, I went to the house to take one last look, hoping it was finally ready for us to move in. As I entered the house. I turned the kitchen doorknob and pushed, but the door wouldn't open. I pushed harder, thinking *sometimes the doors expand in summer because of the heat, but now the weather is cold*. I kept pushing until I felt as if my hand was paralyzed, then I started hitting the door with my shoulder, trying to use my body weight to open it. After a few jolts of pain in my shoulder, the door flew open and banged against the wall. The kitchen was flooded, and the wood of the doors was saturated and swollen. To be sure, this was the reason for the problem, I tried to shut the door again, but there was no way it would fit back in the frame. It didn't take me long to discover the reason for the flooding; water was spurting from around the edges of the ceramics. *Wow, a spring in my kitchen, how lucky am I?*" We both laughed.

He went on, "Well, the plumber came after only two days this time and of course he broke half of the floor tiles to change the damaged pipe. After that I had to bring in a carpenter to fix the doors."

"Congratulations, now you are living in the house with your family, aren't you?" I asked. We were on the Airport Road, only a few minutes before I would drop him off.

"Yes, I would be, if the house was still there," he said with a face full of sorrow.

"You sold it?"

"No, I didn't sell it, but all of this happened just before the war. Once the war started, Kuswa was one of the first areas to come under attack. In the first year of the war, a mortar shell hit the house and completely destroyed it."

I swallowed. I didn't know what the correct response should be in such a situation.

The Mullah noticed my consternation, and said, "Thank God the story has a lucky ending. The house was empty when the mortar hit and we are all still alive."

I was speechless.

We reached the departure level, and I helped the Mullah in with his luggage and bade him goodbye. As I drove back in the direction from which we had come, I couldn't help thinking of how much sorrow people in Syria suffer because of similar situations that happen every day.

Mullah Abdullah al-Allab is the protagonist in The Daughter of Patience.

Baking bread

Firdoo was looking through a loupe at a diamond ring he held between his fingers under the light. The edges were sharp and exact, rather than rounded and dull. Its sparkle was gray and white, not colored. It had inclusions, internal and external flaws. His son Talis was watching him attentively. Firdoo stood up and went to the fridge in the corner of the room. He was living with his son in one room of a three-bedroom shared apartment in Dubai. Not wanting to put their food in the shared fridge in the kitchen, they had bought a secondhand fridge for their own use. Talis was behind him as he opened the fridge, held the ring out in front of the fridge for a few moments, then blew his warm breath on it. Real diamonds don't retain heat well. Firdoo's breath didn't create fog on the gem's surface.

"Good job it's not fake," Firdoo said.

He looked at Talis, with a look that said 'how-did-you-manage-to-steal-it?'

Talis, is in his early thirties, with an athletic body, golden blond hair, and dark green eyes. His striking good looks and masculine charm make it impossible for him to go anywhere without women following him with their eyes.

2: Baking bread

"The black widow was checking out this morning after our night of fun, I simply slipped it into my pocket when I was getting dressed." Talis was a staff member at the Beach Hotel, and one of his duties was to provide special attention to the executive suite whenever it was occupied. It took up the entire thirtieth floor of the hotel and was a unique architectural masterpiece.

"Lucky she didn't notice," his father said.

"She was blinded by love," Talis said, and they both laughed.

"Great. You're really doing great," Firdoo said, "Any new guests in the executive suite this week?"

"Oh, you just reminded me." Talis went to the closet and took out his laptop. It was a third hand laptop still running on Windows Millennium, but it served his purpose. He switched it on and waited a few minutes as it booted up. "This morning, a businessman arrived with his wife. I overheard them yelling at each other. The wife was crying when she stepped out of the hotel limousine." Talis tapped a few keys on the old laptop and stopped to read. His father watched his facial expressions, glad to see a smile on his son's face.

"Where is he from?" Firdoo asked.

"He's originally from India," Talis said, staring at the screen, "Wow, it wasn't a rumor that he arrived from California on his private jet."

"Do you think there's some bread we can bake?" Firdoo asked his son.

"Could be plenty of bread, if we're lucky. According to Uncle Google, this guy owns the company that sells oil refineries to OPEC countries."

"I can smell the fresh bread already," Firdoo said, and they both laughed.

Father and son owned a bakery back in India, but their real work was to smuggle weed and sell it. They would insert cubes of weed in the freshly baked loaves, and business had been great until they were caught. They managed to bribe an official and escaped to start a new life in this massive city.

* * *

Jacob didn't answer his assistant when she called from his holding company's headquarter in Sunnyvale, California. Even though Jacob owned the jet, the long flight from the west coast to this enchanting Middle Eastern city had been draining, so he spent his first day recovering from jet lag. He had come here for two important reasons; first, to finalize an enormous refinery deal with a multinational oil company. The second was to celebrate his six-year anniversary with Lani.

Their first night in the suite, Jacob didn't talk to Lani. Not a single word. He often used this humiliating behavior whenever she defeated him in a discussion using logic. In the morning, Jacob ordered breakfast brought up to the pavilion while Lani went downstairs to the restaurant in the hotel to have her breakfast.

* * *

Lani had first met Jacob following his divorce from his first marriage, which had been an arranged one. She came to his office as a sales executive for an IT company, to sign a service deal. Her manager sent her to meet him because she was from the same hometown as Jacob in India and thought that might help to close the deal. Their relationship moved from professional to personal

2: Baking bread

and Jacob asked her out. One year after their first date they were married in the Noble's Palace in Monaco, with many celebrities and decision makers from around the world in attendance. They honeymooned on a private island in the Maldives. Surely the dream of each and every female on earth, right?

It turned out Lani had married an only child who grew up in an atmosphere of excessive pampering. Lani didn't notice his bad habits until she was living with him under the same roof. Her reaction for the first few months was to remain silent. She told herself these things happened in every family. They were just routine marital problems. She tried to convince herself she was living in bliss. From palaces, to servants, to a private jet to travel wherever and whenever she wanted. Still, any hint of a loving relationship between the couple was just an illusion.

Her husband's behavior got significantly worse as time went on. His tongue did not shrink from uttering insults and hurtful comments. He continually gave her orders, often for silly or meaningless requests. And he demanded immediate satisfaction.

Lani was a well-educated lady, who was used to discussing things logically, accepting things she agreed with and rejecting those she didn't. No one had ever forced her to do anything she didn't wish to do until the day she married Jacob. He now treated her like his property, with no consideration for her feelings. Finally, she could no longer accept his insults in silence. She began putting him down and criticizing him unlike everyone else. This only made his attitude worse, and Lani despaired at ever correcting his behavior. Now, six years later and she's finally made the decision she should have made long ago. She has decided to divorce him, but she hasn't revealed her decision to him yet. Her intention was to inform him on this trip. The euphoria over the great deal her husband is about to sign will make the news of a divorce go easier on him. Or at least, that was her reasoning.

* * *

At 9 am the next morning, Talis was headed for the executive suite, with a steward right behind him pushing the breakfast trolley. Talis paused in front of the carved wooden door with inlaid seashells that led to the executive suite. He dismissed the steward and knocked on the heavy door three times.

This would be the first time Talis laid eyes on the legendary Jacob. Of course, any influential rich people are treated as legends in the online articles, but he can see now, Jacob is a normal human being. He has the same bodily parts every human has. The only difference is the price of clothes he wears and the price of the products he used to wash his ass in the toilet. These details only increase the value of a human being in the eyes of trash people who deserve someone like Jacob to step on their necks.

Talis greeted Jacob politely with a small bow and a warm smile, as he introduced himself without looking him directly in the eye. Jacob didn't answer, just went and sat on the couch, opened the newspaper in front of his face, and resumed his reading.

The suite was open concept, with a jacuzzi in the middle of the living room. A crystal wall and heavy curtains divided the bedroom from the living room. At that moment the curtains were open, and the bedroom was fully exposed.

2: Baking bread

Talis pushed the trolley up to the table, and stood behind it, so the table and the entire apartment were in front of him. That way he wouldn't have his back to anyone sitting in the living area. With expert hands, he uncovered the silver tray which contained a middle eastern style breakfast; hummus, haloumi cheese, falafel, two types of olives, labneh, and fresh mint leaves. As he carried the tray over, his eyes flicked briefly over the Rolex on the tea table in front of Jacob. As he arranged the plates on the table, his eyes also took note of the leather handbag and the handmade Vertu mobile phone ornamented with diamonds. He placed a ceramic pot of hot water on the table, a glass of orange juice, and some small jars of fresh milk, cream, and honey. Meanwhile, his eyes flicked over the open safe in the bedroom, spotting a glittering diamond necklace hanging out of a velvet-covered box. He set a little tray containing eight types of tea sachets, plus a sachet of American black coffee, an Arabic coffee pot, and a basket of hot bread on the table.

"Will there be anything else, Sir?" Talis asked with a small bow.

Jacob responded with a slow headshake as he peered over his newspaper at the gold name tag on Talis' brilliant white Jacket. Talis bowed slightly again with a sweet smile and left.

* * *

Jacob dressed in his finest suit after breakfast and left to start the discussion of contract terms.

The meeting was more than successful and ended with agreement from both sides on all the terms and conditions, and the deal was done before the sun had set. Jacob was overwhelmed with happiness like a kid on Christmas day and returned to the hotel, eager to celebrate.

When he arrived at the suite, before he could put his hand on the gold-plated doorknob, a wailing sound froze him in his tracks. It was Lani crying, but she was also talking at the same time. His legs became paralyzed, and he first thought she had someone in the room with her, but after listening for a moment, he realized she was talking on the phone. He moved closer to the thick door, straining to hear as much as possible without raising suspicions.

… I just cannot tolerate him anymore… Yes… this decision since… very sure… hesitant… anymore… same lawyer… divorce documents… not yet… Maybe… will not… No…

Jacob's head was swimming, his legs would barely support him. He leaned against the wall as a deep stillness surrounded him. He shut his eyes tightly for a moment, swallowed hard, then turned and walked back to the lift.

Making his way down to the bar, Jacob sat at a table in the corner, ordered carbonated water and smoked his cigar. He was disoriented and rapidly sinking into a swamp of self-pity. What he'd heard hurt his pride. He remembered the first time he'd seen Lani. She was the most delicate creature he had ever met; with a perfectly shaped body, an enchantingly pretty face, and dark gray eyes that stirred something inside him. He'd invited her for dinner in Monaco that weekend in his private jet. His surprise was unmeasurable when she rejected his invitation without hesitation or fear that he would cancel the deal between the two companies if she didn't accept. At least that's what he felt at the time.

2: Baking bread

Her excuse was quite simple really, but not easy for him to accept. She told him she never dates any man unless he has the qualities she looked for in a future husband.

Jacob admired her response and respected her principles. He started to see her as more than just a female conquest to satisfy his desires. He thought she might even be the kind of woman he wanted to marry, though he didn't mention that to her at the time. He offered Lani a job opportunity in his company, which she also refused politely, which only served to ignite the flames of his need to be even more at this woman's mercy. He had never been rejected in his life, and Lani's reluctance to date him was a totally new feeling for him. He was excited by the challenge and was even more determined to win her over.

An hour later Jacob left the hotel; the lights of the city lit up the night. As Jacob got in the back seat of a taxi sitting out front of the hotel, he glanced at the driver who appeared to be an old Indian man with a long white beard, with only its edge colored with henna. He had a wrinkled face and wore a round white hat over his white hair. There was something familiar about the old man's face. Maybe his eyes? He wondered about it briefly, then forgot about it.

"Where to sir?" the driver asked, looking at him in the rearview mirror.

"Nowhere special. Just drive please," Jacob said without looking the driver in the eye.

The driver stomped on the fuel pedal, causing the car to jerk forward, and Jacob's head to bounce back, causing a sharp pain in his neck. He merely continued to stare out the window into the night.

"You seem troubled, sir," the driver spoke in Hindi, looking at Jacob again in the rearview mirror. When

Jacob didn't reply, he repeated it in English, however Jacob still didn't reply.

When the car stopped at a red light, the driver turned his head and looked at Jacob, "I will drive on the beach road, so you can release your negative energy to the smell of the sea and the crashing of the waves." The light turned green, and he resumed driving.

Jacob was silent the entire time, so the old driver talked instead, jumping from topic to topic. He talked about the Oscar prize and his opinion that it was a waste of money, then he moved on to informing him how much the municipality struggled to maintain this city's roads, and the reckless younger drivers costing them a fortune to mend the roads after their fatal accidents. He talked about how white the English Queen's teeth were and how she was always smiling to expose those teeth, and he wondered what brand of toothpaste she used to make them so white. He voiced his opinion about the American election, saying it was a sign of the end of the world when a black president moves into the white house. He complained about how much the drivers in this expensive city suffer, because they don't earn enough. Finally, he concluded his commentary with, "Thank God, as long as we've got our health, nothing else matters." He looked again at Jacob and said, "You look in good health, sir. Why all of this worry and silent brooding?"

Jacob glance at the driver from the corner of one eye. "My wife is cheating on me."

The old driver chuckled as if Jacob had told a funny joke. Then he said, "That's not such a big deal."

Jacob spun around in his seat as if he'd been stung by a hornet. Silent and brooding, he was no more. "Not a big deal!" he yelled, "My wife is cheating on me and you say it's not a big deal! Stop right here, let me out."

A sharp squeal erupted from the tires as the driver hit the brakes, causing both Jacob and him to be thrown forward. When the car was stopped, the driver turned to look into Jacob's eyes, a sly smile on his lips, his own eyes glaring back at Jacob, "If my wife cheated on me, I would slaughter her and drink her blood. Back home this noble act is called honor killing." Then he turned his head back, looked at the meter and said, "That will be thirty-five dollars."

Jacob stepped out, threw a fifty-dollar bill on the seat, slammed the door, and stood next to the car thinking for a moment. An idea suddenly sparked in his brain. He opened the passenger door and sat in beside the old driver who was holding his fifteen dollars change in his hand, waiting for Jacob to take it.

"Keep the change," Jacob said while looking in the eyes of the shocked old man. He thought to himself, *should I ask him? Or would it be too big a risk? Well, what will happen if this senile old man goes to the police? Who would believe someone like him?* He decided to take the risk. If it didn't work out, he could just go back to the US and no one would be witness to what was said in this smelly car. "Would you like to have a thousand times this change?" Jacob asked the driver.

The old man opened his mouth in astonishment, "Fifteen thousand dollars," he said, "Who do you want me to kill?"

Jacob was certain that the driver was joking, but he didn't let it go. "My wife."

The old fellow swallowed hard, looking past Jacob in silence for a few moments. Jacob sat there waiting, until the old man finally look back at him and said, "Do I look like a murderer to you?"

"Not at all, you seemed to be a man of chivalry, that's why I am asking you to help me do the honorable thing you talked about." Jacob avoided looking directly in the eyes of the old man, then he opened the car door and stepped out saying, "You know what, just forget it."

The car didn't move. Jacob didn't move. Finally, the old man stepped out of his car, walked around to where Jacob stood, approaching him face to face. Jacob could smell onion on his breath, as he spoke in Hindi, slowly so Jacob would understand, "Tomorrow, a man will approach you at the hotel and will say to you, 'Ask the baker to bake your bread, even if he asks for half of it.' You can safely ask this man anything you want."

Jacob didn't reply, he walked away without even looking back. He walked the streets like a homeless man without any destination. By the time he returned to the hotel, his feet were aching.

Jacob decided he wasn't going to allow Lani to proceed with the divorce under any circumstances. *She won't get one cent from me.* When he entered the suite, she was asleep. He sat at his laptop for a while, answering a few emails with a distracted mind. Finally he lay down and went to sleep, still boiling with rage.

In the morning, he asked Lani to have breakfast with him in the suite, to which she agreed reluctantly, and once again it was Talis who brought the breakfast. Right away Jacob noticed Lani admiring Talis' good looks.

During breakfast, he informed Lani that he hadn't signed the contract yet, as there were still a few terms to be negotiated. Lani seemed sympathetic, but Jacob wondered if her sympathy was genuine. After breakfast,

2: Baking bread

Lani stayed in the suite and he went down to the cigar lounge on the first floor.

"Ask the baker to bake your bread, even if he asks for half of it." Talis said, putting a coffee tray on the small table beside Jacob's chair as he sat reading the morning newspaper.

Jacob swallowed a few times to wet his dry mouth as he folded the newspaper with shaking hands. He looked around him, but no one else was in the room. Talis smiled at him.

"My wife and I need a presentable person to accompany us on the few trips around the city," said Jacob.

"That will be no problem, sir," Talis said with a charming smile, "I will ask the concierge to prepare a list of the best tourism agencies."

"Don't you think I could ask the concierge to do that myself?"

Talis said with a calm straight voice, "Sir, I have a very busy schedule, I can only be away from the hotel in the evenings and some days I have to work the night shift."

"Don't worry about the time, I will speak with the hotel manager and ask him to grant you paid-leave," Jacob said while carefully examining at his neat cuticles and shiny nails. He raised his head and looked directly into Talis' confused face, "If you agree to help me, that is. Of course, that will be in addition to my payment. It would be like making double paid-leave."

"Not possible, sir," Talis said, his eyes showing no emotion, as if they were made of stone, "My services will only be available after my regular working hours. If you want the noble act to be done, those are my terms. I might reconsider though, if you agree to pay me what I ask, cash in advance."

"And that would be?" Jacob asked.

"A 100 K," Talis said, as calmly as if he had been asked the price of a cup of milk tea.

"You will get the money one day in advance." Jacob said. Then inserted his hand into an inner pocket, took out a gold-plated business card case, picked out a card, wrote his temporary mobile number on the back and handed it to Talis, "Tomorrow, at eleven am we will be waiting for you in the lobby."

* * *

Next Morning, Lani was surprised when Talis accompanied them to the Persian restaurant as per Jacob's request. She was a bit annoyed, not because of the presence of Talis, but because Jacob made such a decision without asking her. Jacob informed her that Talis would be accompanying them wherever they went during the rest of their stay in the city. That bit of news made her secretly happy.

The days passed quickly and Talis spent every evening with them like he was their shadow. Lani started to admire this extremely charming young man even more. He would spend time in their suite after he got off duty each day, sometimes playing cards with Jacob. Talis was everything that she found missing in Jacob. He gave her his full attention and treated her as if she was the center of his world. She was sure she even detected a hint of lust for her in his eyes. Lust that Jacob no longer seemed to have towards her. Once, she caught him staring at her breasts. She couldn't tell if he was admiring her body or her diamond necklace.

She was feeling more and more attracted to Talis, despite Jacob seemed ignorance to what was going on, despite that was happening right under his nose.

Sometimes he even left Talis in the suite alone with her. He would excuse himself, saying he had an urgent message waiting at the concierge desk and only he could sign for it.

When Talis confessed his love for her, she was not surprised. However, she wasn't sure if he was really in love with her or if he simply had desires for her and misinterpreted his feelings as love. She didn't respond to him verbally, but every cell of her body showed that she had fallen under the spell of this charming young man.

* * *

"Jacob and Lani are leaving the morning after tomorrow," Talis said while riffling through the bundles of money he had stolen from the suite. He was in his room with his father, drinking hot tea.

"Tomorrow, you will bake his bread," his father said, and they chuckled.

"No, tomorrow we will bake our bread," Talis said, "I will tell Lani that Jacob wants her dead."

"And that he gave you money to kill her," Firdoo said.

"And that I want to run away with her."

"When she sees the money that Jacob gave you, she will decide she must leave him." Firdoo said.

"She has already confessed to me, that she decided to leave him a long time ago," Talis said.

"But Jacob will not allow it, and the only way you'll be able to run away with her, is to kill him." Firdoo said.

"I will tell Lani all of that before we return to the hotel, because Jacob informed me that he won't attend the opera," Talis said.

"So, what will happen after you reach the hotel?" Firdoo asked.

"The plan I agreed on with Jacob, is that after we return from the opera, he will give me the payment in full. Then, he will insist we go have a drink in the bar as a sort of goodbye before they leave the next morning. I will do my best to get out of going, but he'll insist. We'll leave Lani in the suite, and head down to the bar. I'm supposed to leave Jacob for few moments and pull the fire alarm," Talis said, scratching his chin. "You will be waiting in the stairwell, and during the confusion caused by the fire alarm, you're supposed to rush into the suite and shoot her."

Talis continued while pointing his finger between him and his father, "But our plan is slightly different. After Lani and I return to the suite from the opera, Jacob will give me my payment in full. I'll make sure the money he promised me is all there. Then, I'll hit Jacob and tie him up. I'll show Lani the money he gave me to kill her, and then pretend to call the police from my cell phone."

"That's when Officer Firdoo will receive your call," Firdoo said, and they both laughed.

"My call will be the signal for you to call the concierge and ask for me," Talis said, "The concierge won't know where I am, so she will call my mobile phone and tell me that I have a phone call at the front desk. Then I'll leave the suite and pull the fire alarm in the hall. You'll go in and kill them both, gather up the money and jewelry and leave."

"What if something goes wrong? Like I don't receive your call" Firdoo asked.

"If I don't call you, it means I could find another excuse to leave the suite," Talis said, "You will be waiting in the stairwell, when you hear the fire alarm, you just rush to the suite and be sure to kill both of them, no matter what happens."

* * *

The next morning, Jacob informed Lani they would be attending the opera that evening. He knew how much she loved the opera since she used to travel to Vienna every weekend just to attend the famous operas there. He had booked a private balcony in the theater, and of course, Talis would accompany them. As soon as Jacob told her that, she asked enthusiastically, "What time?"

"Seven fifteen this evening. We'll leave the hotel at six thirty."

"That will be fine," Lani said, "I'll be finished my spa appointment around five."

"What are you having done at the spa this time?" Jacob asked.

"A hot stone massage. Would you like to join me? I can book a double room."

"Thank you, but no," Jacob said, "I'm still busy with the terms of this damn contract. It's getting more complex every day."

After her spa treatment, the concierge delivered a message to Lani. She told her Jacob had called at four thirty to inform Lani he would meet her and Talis at the theater at seven.

* * *

Talis and Lani were in the taxi on the way to the opera. Speaking in low voices, they were going over their plans for the evening.

"According to Jacob's plan," Talis said, "Once we return to the suite, he'll give me the money. Then Jacob and I are supposed to go downstairs to the bar and leave you alone. At some point the fire alarm will go off and a man will burst in and…" Talis imitated the firing of a gun, using his thumb and index finger, aimed at Lani's heart, so the driver wouldn't hear.

"Of course, you won't really leave me," Lani said, "You'll just tie him up and call the police, then make him confess that he paid you to…." She made the gesture of a knife slashing her own neck.

"The police will come, and he will be taken to jail. Then we'll be free to go wherever we want, knowing he can't harm us," Talis said.

When they arrived at the opera, Talis threw the money at the driver without looking at him and told him to keep the change.

When they got to their private balcony, Jacob wasn't there yet, but of course, Talis knew Jacob would not be coming. The opera started at seven fifteen sharp.

Talis slowly moved his leg against her leg. Unlike the previous times, she didn't pull it away. He pretended to be concentrating on the opera, but the lust in Lani's eyes inflamed him.

When the opera was over, Talis dialed his father's number and hung up after the first ring. That was the signal for Firdoo to head to the hotel.

When they returned to the suite, Jacob was waiting for them.

* * *

Lani opened the door and entered first, with Talis close behind her. She screamed when she heard a heavy thud

2: Baking bread

and spun around to see Talis collapsed on the floor. She looked up to see Jacob holding a metal rod in his hand.

"Calm down. Help me lift him onto the bed," Jacob demanded.

Lani was crying, unable to believe what was happening. She tried to run for the door, but Jacob anticipated the move, and blocked her way.

"He's a thief and a murderer," Jacob said.

"You are the thief and murderer. He told me that you paid him to kill me," she screamed, pointing to where the money bag was supposed to be. To her surprise, it wasn't there. She looked at the dining table. No bag. She looked at the bed. No bag. Then she looked back at Jacob, who was squatting down beside Talis, holding a diamond necklace in his hand. It was her diamond necklace. She hadn't been able to find it that morning, and Jacob seemed to show concern when she told him. He had promised her he would complain to the hotel manager, as well as the police.

"What do you think about him now?" Jacob asked, his face quite pale.

Lani was confused, not knowing what to answer.

"Don't worry, the police will get a confession out of him, and he'll spend a long time in prison." Jacob said, "Please help me get him onto the bed."

She obeyed and was still crying as Jacob bound Talis' arms and legs with plastic zip ties. She wondered where he'd got those from.

Then Jacob covered Talis with a quilt from head to toe, then called the front desk from the phone beside the bed, "Please may I speak with the manager."

She stared at his back, her head throbbing painfully, her throat dry, and her hands like ice. Jacob turned and looked at her while waiting for the manager to pick up.

"The duty manager? Yes, no problem… It's an urgent matter… yes please…. oh no, it can't wait… what floor is his office on? Ok, thanks."

He hung up the phone and strode to the door. Before he opened it, he turned and looked at her, "Wait for me here. Do not go near him. He is dangerous." He left, slamming the door behind him.

Lani stared at the door as if it might be preventing monsters from entering the room. She was still on the floor when the fire alarm went off. The seconds ticking by seemed like an eternity. The room was spinning crazily. Her heart pounding against her ribs as if it was trying to run away from her chest. She broke into tears again, jumped up and started for the door, then stopped short when it opened suddenly.

* * *

Firdoo put the razor down and stared at the clean-shaven face in the mirror that he hadn't seen in a very long time. He'd been years growing out his white beard, but the sacrifice would be worth it. He was wearing the suit Talis had borrowed for him. Now he combed his hair neatly and put on the Gatsby cap and sunglasses and went out to take a bus to the Beach Hotel. In his pocket was the key card for the door of Jacob and Lani's suite Talis had left for him. Tucked in the inside pocket of his jacket was a gun with a silencer.

He didn't remove the sunglasses when he arrived in the bright lobby, just headed for the thirtieth floor. The bellman called Sami was in the lift. He knew Firdoo, but only with a long white beard. Luckily, he didn't recognize him through his disguise. The bellman exited the lift on the twelfth floor and Firdoo breathed a sigh of relief.

Arriving on the thirtieth floor, he checked the corridor, then peered through the small window of the door to the stairwell. No one there, so he pushed the door open, entered the stairwell and closed the door behind him. He didn't expect to be waiting very long. He just had to wait for the fire alarm to go off, then he would go into action. A few minutes later he heard the suite door slam. It could only be Talis, and a few minutes later the fire alarm erupted. If he hadn't been expecting it, he probably would have had a heart attack.

He put his hand on the gun in his pocket without taking it out, flicked off the safety and placed his finger lightly on the trigger. Leaving the stairwell, he approached the door to the suite. With his left hand, he took out the keycard and touched it to the black screen above the gold knob. The lock clicked, and he pushed the door open. A woman came running and screaming with her hands raised, "Nooo…" her voice was drowned out by the insistent blare of the fire alarm. Three bullets threw her backward, blood splattering on the plush carpet.

As he approached the bed, he could see a body wriggling and groaning under the covers. Without hesitation, he raised the gun and fired three more bullets; the body stopped moving and blood stained the quilt. The alarm continued its deafening trill, but he could hear running feet and voices in the corridor, then a knock on the door and a voice telling him to evacuate immediately. He put the gun back in his pocket and exited the suite, moving toward the stairs where he joined everyone else who was running down.

When he arrived in the lobby out of breath, the concierge apologized to everyone and informed them that one of the guests had pulled the alarm by mistake. The guests were furious, but Firdoo was glad for the false alarm.

* * *

The next morning, Firdoo received a call from the coroner's office asking him to come down and identify his son's body. He had been found dead at the Beach hotel with three bullets in him. Most likely the result of an honor killing, they told him.

3

A mature lady, with enchanting nature,
A mother to many foreigners,
An image of the synergy between three races,
A western style host with Islamic culture,
She is Kuala Lumpur.

Akev

The ceiling fan spun slowly above the four of us. Kuala Lumpur's humidity is more bearable at this time of day. From where we were seated in the living room, I could see the towers in the city center, glowing in the final rays of the sun before darkness closed in once more.

We were gathered around a Ouija board placed in the center of the table. Luna and I had our index fingers resting on a silver Malaysian ringgit; the original planchette had long since gone missing. Mira and Sara were only observers. When the coin moved to the "Yes" circle in the top right corner, we snatched our fingers off as if we'd been burned, and gasped. My ears got hot, and I was sure the other three girls could see them glowing red.

I am the education consultant who enrolled Luna in the dentistry program at a private university, but she'd dropped out and I still hadn't informed her family yet. I was also Sara and Mira's consultant; both of them second-year nursing students.

"Did you move it?" I asked Luna.

"I swear on my mother's head I didn't move it," Luna said and jumped up from the fake leather sofa. The sofa sucked air in audibly, as if it had been suffocating under her weight.

"Ok, ok, calm down. I told you a hundred times not to swear to things. I believe you without swearing." I said, rolling my eyes.

"Did you move it?" Luna asked as she flopped back on the poor sofa.

"No, I did not."

"Both of you are liars," Sara said with a shaky voice.

Mira swallowed deeply, her eyes moving erratically right and left. I looked at Luna. "Are you sure you didn't move it?"

"Would I swear on my mother's head if I did!" Luna yelled. "Let's try one more time."

I put my finger on the silver coin. Luna placed hers next to mine and said, "Is there a spirit in the room?"

Nothing happened, and the four of us exhaled. Luna pulled her finger away. Suddenly the coin moved a little and stopped. In the heavy silence, Luna placed her finger back next to mine and said again, "Is there a spirit here with us?" The coin moved to Yes. To be sure, I moved the coin back to the center of the board and Luna asked again. The coin moved to Yes.

Sara was one of those dedicated children who had spent years memorizing the verses of the Qur'an from cover to cover. She started reciting Qur'anic verses out loud. Mira covered her mouth with her right hand, as if she was looking at a dead body.

It was very exciting for me because I had never believed in a Ouija board. I ignored Sara and Mira's horror and took the lead since I was the oldest.

"Are you male or female?"

The coin moved slowly to "M."

To be sure, I asked, "Are you male?"

The coin moved to Yes.

"How old are you?"

The coin moved to 3, then 5, then 7. Both Luna and I gasped, and to confirm, I asked, "You are 357 years old?"

The coin moved to Yes.

"What is your name?"

The coin moved to A, K, E, and V.

"Akev," Luna, Mira, and I whispered.

"Are you Muslim?" I asked.

The coin moved to No.

"Are you Christian?"

The coin moved to No.

"Are you Jewish?"

The coin moved to Yes.

"Do you live with us in this house?"

The coin moved to Yes.

Mira gasped. Tears started to run down her thin pink cheeks, while Sara continued to recite the Qur'an loudly. I continued my questions.

"Are you the only spirit staying here with us?"

The coin moved to Yes.

Luna asked, "Do you stay in my room?"

The coin moved to No. Luna exhaled in relief.

"Do you stay in Sara's room?"

The coin didn't move. I looked at Sara; her face was pale, with a mix of emotions that I couldn't interpret. Fear or sorrow or anger, or a mix of them all? She stopped reciting for few seconds, and then as if she had been injected with adrenaline, she resumed even louder and more forcefully with her eyes shut tightly.

The coin moved to No.

Mira and I swallowed.

"Do you stay in Mira's room?" I asked.

The coin moved immediately to No.

There was only my room left.

3: Akev

"Do you stay in my room?"

The coin moved to No.

I realized I had been holding my breath. I exhaled.

Sara still had her eyes shut, and the three of us looked at each other, confused. We wondered where on earth Akev stayed, if not in our rooms. Then I remembered that some types of jinni like to live in bathrooms.

"Do you stay in the bathroom?" I asked and then stuttered, "A... Akev."

The coin moved to No.

"Do you stay in the living room?"

The coin moved to No.

"Do you stay in the kitchen?" The kitchen was on the left after entering the house, so nearest to the outside door.

The coin moved to Yes.

"Are you happy to talk to us?" I asked.

The coin moved to No.

Sara yelled "Allah Akbar" and Mira gasped and stood up and ran to her room, slamming the door forcefully.

"Can we call you again sometime, Akev?" I asked.

The coin moved faster than ever to No.

* * *

From that day onward, nothing was ever the same again.

My apartment was on the thirty-eighth floor in the Boleh Condominium in Kuala Lumpur, where I had been living for three years. I worked in the education agency, enrolling hundreds of students from around the world in Malaysian universities. Most of my students live in this same condominium since I have a contract with the housing company. For the apartment where I live, I chose only females.

After the Ouija experience, every time Luna, Mira, and I enter the apartment, we look toward the kitchen and call out, "Hello, Akev!" just to tease Sara, who had been unable to live normally in the apartment once she knew we had a jinni. She wanted to move out, but her parents wouldn't agree. They believed their daughter would be safer with me.

I only saw the girls at night, after work. We would gather in the living room, smoke a hookah, and chat happily. Most of the time it was me, Mira, and Sara, plus whichever girls we decided to invite that day. Boys were not allowed. Luna locked herself in her room most of the time, especially since she'd stopped attending university.

One weekend, twelve female students and I went to Batu cave at the outskirts of Kuala Lumpur. Afterwards we returned to the apartment to enjoy the Kabsah, Luna had cooked for us, while we were away visiting the cave. Despite her many shortcomings, she was an amazing cook. When we sat down to eat, I discovered we had only seven spoons. I asked, "Where are the other five spoons? We should have twelve, I bought them myself." My question was drowned out by the chatter and only Luna and Sara, the ones nearest to me, heard me.

"Akev ate them," Luna said, teasing Sara.

Sara threw down her spoon and stomped off to her room, slamming the door behind her.

The room got very quiet, as the visiting girls looked to me, Mira, and Luna for an explanation. Luna told them about the Ouija and Akev living in our kitchen.

I don't think they believed her because they made a few sarcastic remarks and forgot all about it within a few minutes. I soon dismissed it from my own mind, and we ate our meal with disposable plastic spoons.

One morning, a few days later, I wanted to fry eggs, but the pan was missing. I decided not to stress about it. Maybe someone had taken it to their room during the night. When I returned that evening, I asked about it, but no one seemed to know the whereabouts of the pan.

The next day, I ordered new utensils and two new pans online.

One evening two weeks later, I was enjoying the view of the skyline from the living room windows. From this height the glittering twin towers and the newly built high rises surrounding them looked like a group of fashionable ladies wearing elegant night dresses. Mira and Sara were enjoying the view as well, so we switched off the lights to make the view even clearer. I often like to pretend I'm the queen of the city from my throne high in the sky.

"It's been two weeks since I ordered those pans," I said, "I wanted to cook noodles, after work, but there were no forks or spoons, and now one of the two pans we had left is missing, along with one of the old pots, and half of our plates are gone as well."

Luna came out her room and joined the discussion, switching on the lights as she did so. She smelled really bad. Mira, Sara and I looked at each other but didn't say anything.

"You know me, I don't cook at home, I always eat at the university," Mira said.

I looked at Sara, but she only shook her head without commenting.

I looked at Luna, who does the most cooking at home and always eats in her room. She blurted out, "I think Akev is stealing our stuff."

"Be serious," Sara snapped.

"How are you managing to cook?" I asked Luna.

"I just use whatever is clean in the kitchen," she said.

"There must be someone taking these things. They don't just disappear by themselves," I said.

"As far as I know, only the cleaning maids have keys so they can come in and clean when we're not in," Sara said. The housing office sends maids to clean the common areas, but we clean our own rooms ourselves.

"The maids have never changed since I moved into this apartment. These disappearances never happened before," I said.

"At least not until Akev introduced himself," Luna said, and giggled with Mira.

Next morning, I complained to the management at the housing office. Since I've brought them plenty of tenants, they took the matter seriously, and without asking for further evidence they agreed to change the maids for our building.

I bought new utensils, pots, and pans for the kitchen, but they too disappeared one by one. A few other things started to disappear as well. After each cleaning, the maids leave two black plastic trash bags for us to use during the week until they return to clean again. Even the trash bags disappeared. The cockroach spray disappeared, and so did the air freshener.

The idea of a jinni living in our kitchen was absurd enough, but the conclusion arrived at by the three girls living with me in the apartment was even weirder. They were all starting to believe that Akev was taking the stuff.

It all came to a head one evening. A big argument broke out about changing apartments. Either that or we had to find a way to get Akev to leave. It wasn't a big

3: Akev

problem for me, the missing utensils, plates, pans, or pots. The big problem was the loss of our day-to-day peace of mind. Our apartment had always been a hub for our friends to spend pleasant times together and sleep over.

Gradually that changed. Now Sara was always arguing with Luna, who teased her day and night that Akev sometimes spent nights in her room watching her sleep. That was too creepy to even imagine.

I promised them I would speak with the housing office to find a different apartment for us to move to, but we agreed we wouldn't move until after I returned from my business trip to China.

I left two days later and promptly forgot about the matter of changing apartments. I was away for two weeks, negotiating agreements with several education agencies. During my stay in China, I received a call from the housing office asking why Luna hadn't paid her rent yet for the current month, and why she wasn't responding to their text messages or phone calls. It was the fifth of the month and she was supposed to pay no later than the second. I promised the manager to follow through to find out the reason and let them know as soon as possible.

After I hung up the phone, I called Luna, but her mobile phone was turned off. I texted her, asking her to call me as soon as possible. Luna's parents had informed me she has an anxiety disorder and I should keep her under close observation. It worried me at times because people with anxiety disorder sometimes commit suicide. I was beginning to feel she might be suffering more than an anxiety disorder. She was acting like someone with deep depression. I texted Mira and asked about Luna. She got right back to me, saying that Luna had gone back to her home country due to a death in the family. That set my mind at ease. At least she wasn't lying dead in her room! I texted her parents to inquire about her. No reply.

Due to my busy schedule, I didn't give the matter any further thought and few days passed before I received a text message from the housing office informing me they would be preparing Luna's room for a new tenant. I knew that they were not asking me and even if I objected, they wouldn't listen unless I paid her rent myself and I wasn't about to do that.

A few hours later, I received some photos from the housing office.

One photo showed a dresser piled high with dirty pots and pans. It appeared as if they'd been used for cooking and had never been washed or even emptied out. They were piled all over the dresser, with cockroaches swarming between the piles, as if they were having a party and enjoying the rotting food. Another photo showed a dirty yellow stained mattress on a bare floor. Piled all around it were the broken parts of the bedframe.

Photos of the bathroom showed piles of black trash bags and dirty, wet clothes. A few photos showed walls that had originally been white or cream; now they had large patches of greenish gray on them. A photo of the closet showed piles of dirty knives, forks, and spoons.

I shut my eyes tight and breathed deeply. The photos were clear enough. I knew it was Luna's room, but I was hoping someone would tell me I was wrong, so I texted back, "Where were these taken?"

The answer I received was, "Luna's room, and the smell in there is beyond belief."

The Power of Words

Tick... tock... tick... tock...
The clock hands stopped at eleven minutes after eleven.

The tip of the pen froze in place over the period after the last word of the last sentence of the last line. The paralysis worked its way up the pen, spreading up the arm and then through the body of the writer as steadily as ice crystals in a flash freezer. The words that had come out of the now frozen pen started to vibrate on the white page, one by one popping up as they changed from two dimensions to three, as if they'd been pumped up like a balloon, ready to burst at the first touch.

The first word that popped out of the white surface was the title at the top of the page. It landed vertically on the paper and stretched its limbs while looking at the rest of the words, now popping like popcorn off the surface to land vertically across the page, without changing their positions, so the sentences were still comprehensible.

The words were talking, screaming, shouting, and arguing with each other like people in a public bath when the shower water stops flowing while they still have shampoo foam on their heads and faces.

"Quiet!" *Title* yelled, forcing all the words to fall silent and look at him. He continued talking with his British accent, "We can't help our master if we act in an uncivilized manner. We must be united."

Title looked at the words spread out before him. They were waiting for him, so he asked *Adjective*, "Will you kindly explain the situation to us?"

"Indeed," *Adjective* said, "We need to act fast before our creator goes on farther in the story. We don't want the disaster of the Muddy Days novel to happen again. He wrote a hundred and fifty thousand words that time, without realizing the deadly holes in the plot. To make matters worse, his editor didn't address the holes either. He simply told him to start a new book because his mistakes were unsolvable."

"Oh, Pen," *Adverb* said and fainted on the smooth surface of the paper.

"Bloody drama queen," *Verb* said.

The words panicked again and started to talk and argue all at the same time.

"Enough," *Title* snapped in a voice that allowed for no option except obedience. He looked up at the frozen eyes of the writer, and sighed, "His daughter's disease is eating away at his mind, his wife is away overseas, and the final notice came from the landlord today, ordering him to evacuate the house if he doesn't pay the last three months' rent."

The loud sobbing of *Preposition* drew the attention of all words, who stared at her all collapsed in a heap and crying her eyes out.

Title rolled his eyes, then continued what he was saying. "Our master is overwhelmed by stress."

"But he still must deliver the manuscript on time, or it will be a disaster," *Adjective* said, then muttered under its breath, "Oh, dear Pen."

3: *The Power of Words*

Title turned scarlet when he saw *Pronoun* moving around the other words, leaving his spot in the sentence vacant. *Title's* scream startled all the words, causing them to jump in their spots, "*Pronouuuuun*, get back to your own bloody spot!"

Pronoun said, "Oh, dear Pen," and avoided meeting the glares of the other words, as he jumped back to his spot.

All the words started talking noisily again, as if they were attending a party.

Title spoke with clenched teeth, "I am the title of an eighty-thousand-word novel. I don't have all day to waste. Everyone please focus."

"We must find a logical solution," *Verb* said.

"Bloody exotic advice, that," *Noun* said.

Some words laughed, and some looked at *Noun* as if he'd spit on the clean white paper.

"I agree with *Verb*, we should think of a logical way to help our master," *Adjective* said.

"And make this novel a best seller," *Noun* said.

"Are you serious?" *Verb* looked at *Noun* with pity. "If he was talented enough, one of his previous five novels would have been a best seller and he wouldn't be drowning in shit like this. He can't even afford to fix his ancient typewriter."

"I think he should just get a job as a shoe repairman," *Pronoun* said, but he was the only one who laughed.

"Our fellow words from the self-improvement books always tell stories of the many composers who never gave up and became best sellers in the end," *Noun* said.

"Yes, then there's the lady who wrote some books about a wizard. She didn't find an agent for her first book until she was writing the last book in the series," *Adjective* added.

83

"She was writing book number seven, not book number two hundred," *Verb* said.

"Our master is writing book number six, not two hundred," *Adjective* said.

"Not only writers," *Noun* said, "My cousin who lives in a motivational book told me about an old man who built a theme park. He said the old man went broke nine times before he accomplished his dream."

"Then there's the guy who discovered the magical orange light in the glass bulb hanging from the ceiling," *Adjective* said. "He tried nine hundred and ninety-nine materials before finding the correct one."

"They call it electricity," *Verb* said.

"Whatever," *Adjective* said without looking in the direction of *Verb*, "There is the guy who invented the secret recipe for the smelly fried chicken our composer eats. It's said he entered hundreds of shops, promoting his recipe until he found someone interested in buying it from him, and now millions of people eat his recipe every day."

"Ok, there are plenty of stories proving your point," *Verb* said, glaring at *Adjective*.

"My fellow words, we must not waste any more time. We need to try to find a solution," *Title* said.

"Our Master is being cold in this novel; emotionless descriptions, weak sentences, a dull plotline, plenty of redundant words, etc." *Verb* said, then asked no word in particular, "Am I right?"

"Yes, you are," *Noun* said.

"So what do you advise?" *Adjective* asked *Verb*.

Verb looked at *Adjective* and asked, "Is there a logical solution?"

"Let's hear some suggestions and I'll tell you which one is the most logical," *Adjective* said.

"I advise him to fictionalize what he is going through and write it down so his novel will have deep emotions," *Verb* said.

All the words looked at *Verb,* anticipating more ideas, but *he* was apparently finished.

"Wow, one suggestion. Doesn't anyone else have ideas for solving the problem?" *Noun* asked.

"What should we do, what should we do, what should we do?" *Preposition* yelled, slapping her own face while running around erratically.

"Oh, dear Pen," *Title* said, and yelled out, "Enough." causing every word to freeze where they were. *Then he* asked no word in particular, "Any of you have anything to say?"

"Our lord Pen help us find a solution and help our composer to write again," *Adverb* was mumbling with her eyes tightly shut and her hands pressed together in front of her mouth.

"Can you help?" *Title* asked *Verb*, "You're the one who finds the solution every time."

"We have plenty of wiser words than I, among us," *Verb* said in a deep husky voice.

"No need to try to impress us with your humbleness now," *Noun* said.

A few words shot angry looks at *Noun*.

"Well, despite what you say, you've always given the best solutions in the past," *Title* told *Verb*.

"In that case, I am your humble servant, and ask you to consider changing the order of the words in all the sentences you disagree on and make them acceptable, just like what we did in 'The Silky Milky Thread'."

"Our genius master thinks he's Leo Tolstoy," *Adverb* said.

"In 'The Silky Milky Thread' we messed up when we changed the order of the words." *Noun* Said, "Most of our reader reviews complained about unclear meaning and redundant phrases. I don't think we should try the same trick in this novel, because not one of us has a brain like our composer to guarantee the sentence quality while changing the order of the words."

All the words turned to stare at *Pronoun*, who was running around franticly yelling, "What do we do, what do we doooooo?"

Title darted out in front of him and slapped him, hard. *Pronoun* fainted on the white smooth surface of the paper.

"Anyone else need a good slap?" *Title* screamed.

All the words swallowed, but no one commented.

Title looked sternly at *Verb* and asked him in a normal voice, "What do you think we should do?"

Verb was thinking deeply, as he looked at the huge tip of the pen poised over the period, as if he might get inspiration from it. All the words were looking at him expectantly.

"The protagonist travels to Russia to meet his secret lover, leaving his wife and son back in London. While he's in Russia, his mistress is murdered…" *Verb* said to no one in particular, "… then, what if the son back in London, develops the same disease as our master's daughter? Then the protagonist will feel guilty and decide to be loyal and faithful to his family back in London, but it was too late because he was the main suspect of the murder." All the words were observing *Verb* attentively while he was narrating the rest of the story and he concluded, "I believe readers will read between the lines and feel our master's deep emotions coming through his words."

"It sounds good," *Title* said and then asked, "*Adjective*, what do you say? Is that a logical solution?"

"Yes, very," *Adjective* said.

"What do you say, *Noun*?" *Title* asked.

"I say it's good, but let's get the opinion of the majority," *Noun* said.

Title waved his hand at him, as if he was shooing a fly.

"Let's vote," *Noun* yelled, looking around at the group.

"Let's vote, let's vote," all the words chanted together.

"Ok, ok, let's vote," *Title* gave in. "Who agrees with *Verb's* solution?"

All the words raised their limbs.

"Well than, its unanimous. Let's fix the book! Here we go," *Title* said. All the words cheered and did a little dance in celebration.

Title dove back into the white paper like diving into a swimming pool. The rest of words imitated him, and the surface of the paper became smooth once again; covered with two-dimensional letters.

Tick… tock… tick… tock

The writer put down the pen, stretched luxuriously, like a cat awaking from a long nap, and headed for the kitchen to fix a cup of coffee.

Bedtime Story

"Have a seat please," my supervisor said as I entered his office. He had asked me to see him after our sales meeting in the showroom. His office overlooks the showroom and all the shiny new cars on display there.

"Thank you, Sam," I said, unbuttoning the six buttons of my suit jacket before sitting down. Sam looked at me with the eyes of a patient father. He was younger than me, but in the new car sales business your position is decided by your results, not your age or fancy degree.

"I would like to congratulate you on your results once again. The announcement at the meeting was the official one. This one is my personal congratulations." Sam's wide smile showed off his immaculate white teeth. I guess his earnings allow him to purchase veneers.

"I appreciate that, Sam," I said, my head held high.

"I don't want to keep you long," Sam said, smoothing his impeccably clean silk tie, as if he'd noticed an atom of dust on it. "As you know, next week is our company's anniversary celebration. Many hard-working salespeople will be receiving awards," then he whispered, while looking right and left, "You will be one of them."

"I appreciate the honor, Sam, but why wouldn't you keep that as a surprise? Why are you telling me this now?"

He sighed, "Because I want to caution you not to wear this suit to the anniversary celebration." Before I could say anything, he raised his right hand, palm facing me, "I know, I know, it's your father's suit. Your Mother gave it to you as a birthday gift. You've told everyone in the office that, but the CEO will be presenting you with an award, and I don't want him to see you in this outdated suit. You're earning twice the amount of your six colleagues in this showroom. For heaven's sake, buy a new suit."

I nodded my head as I stood and buttoned up my jacket, "All right, Sam. Will there be anything else?"

"No, you're free to go, and thank you again." He nodded to me, then turned back to his computer screen.

* * *

I parked the BMW in front of my house. The same house where I had grown up with my father. I have many fond memories with my father, but no memories at all with my mother. She's in a nursing home now, where the staff takes good care of her. They're experts, specially trained to deal with people like her. As I entered the house, Matthew, wearing his Spiderman overalls, ran and tried to jump up on me. I bent down, scooped him up, and gave the five-year-old a big hug.

"How's my little bear?" I asked him, kissing him on the top of his head.

He just giggled as I put him down, and I went to the kitchen where my wife Mona was putting the final touches on dinner. I inhaled deeply the aroma of shrimp fried in batter. She was pouring the contents of a pan over a bowl of penne pasta. I kissed her, then went upstairs to wash up and change my clothes. I came down to find Mona and Matthew sitting at the table waiting for me.

We settled in to enjoy our dinner, but just like my father, I demanded silence at the dinner table. He always said it was disrespectful to talk while your mouth was full of food, or while others were eating. I love Matthew unconditionally, like my father did me. But with a five-year-old boy at the table, enforcing the rule was nearly impossible. Matthew would get distracted, playing with his fork and spoon as if they were robots fighting over the pasta, then the winning robot would attack a shrimp and pop it in his mouth. He was killing us laughing at him. That is, until Mona noticed that pasta and shrimp were flying off the plate onto the table and even some landing on the floor. She took the pretend robots from him and proceeded with dinner, putting one spoonful in her own mouth followed by one in Matthew's.

After dinner, Mona helped Matthew brush his teeth before sending him to his room to change and get ready for bed. Later, I told Mona about the conversation with Sam. I was expecting her to be on my side, but she agreed with Sam that I should stop wearing the outdated suit. That was hurtful. She knows how much I value my mother's gift, especially since it belonged to my father. I didn't want to argue, so I just nodded.

When I went to Matthew's room to read him a bedtime story, he was under the covers waiting for me with a smile that almost caused my heart to stop beating.

"How's my little bear?" I asked.

Matthew just giggled.

"What story does my little bear want to hear?" I asked, but I already knew the answer, because it was the only story he ever asked for.

3: Bedtime Story

"*The Herder and the Cow*," Matthew said.

It was a bedtime story my father used to tell me, and I had continued the tradition with Matthew. It never failed me. As always, before I reached the end, Matthew would be asleep with the same innocent smile every kid has, knowing their father is there.

"... When the herder brought the goblet of water to his father, he found the old man had fallen asleep again..."

Most nights by this point Matthew would be breathing deeply, fast asleep. Tonight, for some reason he was still wide awake.

"The herder didn't want to wake his father up, but he didn't want to leave him either. What if his father woke up and didn't find the water to drink?"

"Daddy, why didn't he leave the water beside his father and go back to sleep?" Matthew asked.

"That would have been considered impolite in those days," we said together and laughed.

Matthew pulled himself up enthusiastically and said, "Daddy, if you asked me to get water for you in the middle of the night," he made some choking noises that most kids make when they try to talk and breathe at the same time, "and when I came... when I came in your room, I found you sleeping." More noisy breathing, then he continued, "I will... I will wait for you until morning, like the herder did for his father." His words brought tears to my eyes.

"My dad always told me this story before I went to sleep, and I always told him just what you said."

"Daddy, did you have a cow?" he asked, being very serious.

"No, I didn't."

He slid under the quilt again and I continued the story, remembering the green book my father read this story from.

"… When the old father woke up in the morning, he found his son standing there, still holding the goblet as he waited. The son was extremely tired but didn't want his father to know, so he just told his father that he was going to the cattle market for the fifth day in a row, to try to sell their skinny yellow cow. His father raised his hands and asked God to send buyers to his son. When the son reached the market, a group of men paid him the cow's weight in gold…"

"If I waited for you until morning holding a glass of water, I don't want a cow to be full of gold like the herder," Matthew said with genuine concern on his face.

"What would you ask for?" I asked.

"I want a new bicycle!" he said, as he jumped up from the bed again.

"Hey, little bear, where are you going?"

"I am going to bring water for you and wait for you until morning, like the herder." I caught up with Matthew, hugged him tight, and put him back in his bed, which was painted blue and red with a Spiderman decal on the headboard. I covered him with the quilt, kissed his forehead, and said, "Your daddy doesn't want you to bring him water just so I'll buy you a new bicycle." I switched the light off and before closing the door, I said, "Sleep tight, my little bear."

"What about the bicycle?" Matthew asked.

"On the weekend we'll go look at bicycles, now go to sleep," I said, and closed the door.

* * *

At the breakfast table next morning, before I left for work, Mona asked me, "Darling, are you free on Friday evening?"

3: Bedtime Story

"Why, what's on your mind?" I asked, raising a spoonful of cereal to my mouth. I listened to her response while munching the crunchies.

"They're giving a free seminar at the YMCA for people who faced challenges during their childhood. Sometimes, as a defense mechanism, they invent their own version of their history in their mind."

"Darling, as far as I know, you had the best childhood a kid could ever wish for. Why would you need to go to such a seminar?"

"No reason. Just networking and making new friends." Her forehead furrowed as she stared blankly at the mug held in between her hands.

"I'm not interested," I said while swiping through emails on my smart phone screen. "You go and have a great time. Matthew and I will come to pick you up after, and we can go for ice cream together. That was another tradition my father followed every Friday evening."

"Sounds great," she said, without looking me in the eye.

"I don't know why my mom never came with us on those outings. I'm very glad we're always together when we go out with Matthew."

* * *

Friday evening, while waiting for Mona to finish her seminar, Matthew and I went to the bookshop in the mall next to the YMCA. Matthew was enjoying his time in the kids' section, I was in the novel section, with one eye on Matthew and one eye reading the descriptions on various books and flipping through their pages, enjoying the smell of the paper. While I was flipping the pages of a murder mystery novel, Matthew came running to me, carrying a green story book.

"Look, Daddy!" Matthew raised the book high for me to see.

My heart thumped against my ribs. It was the same book my father used to read from. I took it and opened it, enjoying the familiar illustrations. Matthew stood watching me.

I opened the cover, looking for the amazing book's publisher. Then my eyes fell on the date of its first publication. Taking Matthew's hand, I paid for the book and we left to pick up Mona.

"Are you alright darling?" My wife asked, staring at me when she got in the car. "You look unwell."

"Matthew my little bear," I said, "Please pass me the story book I bought for you," I took it without removing my eyes from the road. Handing it to Mona I said, "Please open and tell me what year it was published."

"This book was first published in 1985. So what?"

"My dad passed away in 1975."

"What are you talking about?"

"This is the book my father used to read my bedtime story from, don't you get it?"

"Are you sure?"

I stared at her without saying a word. She turned her head, avoiding my eyes.

The ice-cream was great, but Mona and I were silent the whole time. The only sounds came from Matthew, who was busy preventing aliens from eating his ice cream.

* * *

Monday after work, I didn't head home directly. Instead, I went to see my mother at the retirement home. It was

3: *Bedtime Story*

a thirty-minute drive from my work. It was only an average retirement home since I couldn't afford a better one. After I parked, I picked up the little green story book and headed inside. I signed in at the reception area and walked to my mother's room. The air was saturated with the smell of disinfectant.

Mom was sitting on a chair in front of the window, overlooking a vast parking lot and a busy highway. *What an exotic view*, I thought. Her eyes were closed, her fingers intertwined, her hands resting on a blanket spread over her lap. I still hadn't said anything when she opened her eyes and looked at me. Deep wrinkles in her face and the sadness in her eyes spoke of many long years of suffering.

I've been busy and rarely visit my mom. It's been only twice this year. Our visits are usually limited to; Hi, how are you? How's Mona? How's Matthew? But today I had a few questions I wanted to ask her. After she asked me about Mona and Matthew, she went back to staring out the window into the void.

The silence was as sharp as razors cutting through my ears. I looked around. Her room was so simple; a single bed, a cupboard, and the chair she was sitting on. The only TV was in the common room where residents could sit if they wanted to watch.

"Mom, do you remember this?" I asked, as I held out the green book to her.

She squinted at the book without touching it. She just looked at me, waiting for more explanation.

I pulled my arm back and said, "This is the book dad used to read my bedtime story from, when I was little."

She just stared at me.

"You don't remember, do you?"

"I am not senile, yet."

"Don't you remember how much I used to enjoy those bedtime stories?"

"Is this some kind of joke?" she asked, turning her head towards the window.

"Not at all," I said, "but I am confused. That's why I'm asking you. The publishing date of this book was after my father died." I opened the cover and pointed at the year while moving closer to her. She didn't look at the number, she just stared at me as if I was crazy.

"You know when your father died?" she asked, "Do you even know who your father was?"

I was speechless.

"You silly boy, I am a single mother. I knew your father for only half a day. We met on a school trip.

"No, no, no," I was shaking my head.

"I don't even remember what he looked like." She sighed.

"But, what about the suit you gave me for my birthday? You told me it was my father's."

"I didn't say whose suit it was," she said, "I couldn't afford to buy you a new suit, so I bought a second-hand one."

That's the moment when I remembered Mona and the seminar.

4

An elegant lady, with modern ideas,
A mother of thirty million and welcoming more,
A miraculous portrait of accuracy and discipline,
A newly written novel with traditional Chinese characters,
She is Shanghai.

The Writer

I've made my fortune from smuggling books. Sixty-four years ago, the Central Council, which was known back then as the United Nations, decided to make some serious regulations to protect the environment and began to implement them by force. One of these regulations prohibited the production of paper. Printing, in all its forms, was forbidden, and every book, magazine, and newspaper became digitized.

A huge tax was placed on the trade of existing print material. This was intended to minimize the desire in people's hearts to own actual books. As a result, the value of existing books rose sky high.

I was a risk taker and a bold gambler, so I sold my house, moved back in with my parents, and started buying tons of magazines, journals, newspapers, and of course, books; both fiction and nonfiction. At first, I traded them legally here in the United States, choosing not to export because of the enormously high taxes from both sides; as an importer and exporter. But when the government began to levy taxes on trading books, even between the states, I decided to start smuggling them out of the country, because at the end of the day, I saw myself as a servant to knowledge, and wanted to educate people. In order to do that, a few hundred humans were sacrificed during the process, though I convinced myself I was doing nothing wrong. After all, I built my financial empire from smuggling books. Eventually I had depleted all the printed products from the stores, only leaving a few hundred books in my private library.

The world was going through huge changes then, as nuclear power became the prime source of power. The fear of a nuclear emergency and the resulting pollution grew day after day. People became desperate for clean cities to live in, so I built the first shielded town on land reclaimed from the ocean. The business was not very successful until the nuclear disaster happened, resulting in the deaths of three billion people and the destruction of fifty-two major cities. The Central Council prohibited the building of any new buildings on land unless it was deserted. Of course after the nuclear disaster the deserted land was not suitable for human occupation. The only solution was to utilize the seas and oceans. Instead of 70% of earth's surface being covered by water, let it be 60% and let the other 10% be for new cities. However, the land reclamation caused a problem with rising sea levels and as a result, a few islands and shoreline communities were forced to build crystal shields to prevent the water from swallowing their land.

For instance, the occupied islands of Maldives are now totally under the sea, enclosed in crystal domes, allowing people to live inside, like an aquarium. They are fascinating islands that have become an ideal place for tourists to observe ocean life from close up. Nowadays, I have nine hundred twenty-three cities built on artificial islands in the ocean. I also own the factories that produce the shields for cities and islands affected by the rising of the sea. I am one of the three most powerful humans on earth.

The second is Gustilo from Moscow, the owner of the genes factory. He's the one responsible for perfecting all the humans conceived these days. He eliminated the deficiencies in DNA and kept only the pluses. The third is Wang from Shanghai, the owner of the giant space travel company in charge of transporting humans between earth and our colonies in the far reaches of space. The three of us have been key motivators in the progress game, and no one dares to oppose us. I think Gustilo and Wang are decent men, just like me, who did their best to reduce the number of human lives sacrificed during our operations.

I have three sons and two daughters and twenty-seven grandchildren, who now range in age from nine years old to thirty-six. My eldest son is sixty-nine years old now and I am ninety-five, so you can imagine what I look like.

I am sitting on a red leather chair in my room, behind a nine-meter wide, black crystal desk, since wood is no longer available. The chairs are made of marble, covered with luxurious leather cushions. The walls are lined with books on crystal shelves; all the books I have read in my life and I still reread some of them from time to time. To have an actual library is a major offense. Actually, a few presidents ask me from time to time, to borrow from it. That's the reason the Central Council has always pretended they don't know about my library. The only space without books is in front of the windows.

The floor is made of blood red marble, and there are four leather chairs around a rose-colored crystal table. The light comes from two crystal balls floating in the air. One is called sun and the other moon. They imitate the actual sun and moon, one supplying light during the day and the other at night. I am not a sunologist

4: *The Writer*

or a moonologist so I don't fully understand the mechanism involved. I do know there is another sun and moon hovering over the house from which the suns and moons inside derive their power. The two outside derive their power from the actual sun and moon, so even if I ask the sun to light during the night, it won't respond because the sun is not shining outside.

You may already know there is no use of electricity anymore, and no electronic devices either. New devices these days are powered by photonics. Just like the moon and sun in my room, every device on earth now works by utilizing the energy of light. This revolutionary technology was developed after the nuclear disaster fifty years ago.

I place a cigar between my lips, flick my lighter and draw in deeply, feeling the warm silky sensation of the smoke crawling through my lungs. Then I blow it out into the room, enjoying the exotic aroma of this fine Cuban cigar. I think to myself; *This is the life. Of all the things they've banned, a good Cuban cigar is the one I'll miss the most.*

My granddaughter Suzan enters the room with her cousins, Lisa and Farah. They are in their twenties and very dear to my heart. The three of them approach and kiss me on the forehead, causing my heart to flutter. They are the image of perfection. They take their seats and pause to look at one another before Suzan asked me, "Grandpa, do you know a famous composer named Dink Reenlist?"

My heart skips a beat and believe me at my age that can be dangerous. I lower my cigar and tell her, "I am the one and only famous Dink Reenlist, but I am not a composer." Suzan fluttered her eyelashes, as if she was hearing her lover's voice.

"I was a writer before writers became extinct," I said.

"What is a writer?" Farah wanted to know.

I pointed to the books on the shelves, "The people who composed these books were called writers, but when printing was banned, the word was forbidden to be used and writers became extinct." I raised my cigar again and drew on it deeply while squinting at the three amazed granddaughters who are now staring at me as if I'm a legendary astronaut of the last primitive American spaceship. "Why do you ask?"

Suzan took her crystal ring off and laid it on the table. This tiny ring is the most sophisticated device so far; the replacement for primitive phones, computers, cameras, and whatever other electronic devices people used to carry. A rectangle of green light appears above the ring, large enough for me to read the words on the lage; that's short for light page. Suzan says, "I was reading the new edition of the *Sky of Knowledge* and there's an article with a weird title 'Self-Published Writer' and it was composed by Dink Reenlist a long time ago. It was in their photonics archive."

This time my heart skipped two beats. I put the cigar down and hoped my granddaughters didn't notice, but I was too late. The three of them were staring at their legendry grandfather's shaking hands. My eyes filled with tears, and I turned my chair around, so my back was to the three of them. I asked in a husky voice, "Can you read the article to me, my dear Suzan?"

I love listening to my granddaughter's velvety voice, and I squeezed my eyes shut, hanging on every word leaving Suzan's lips.

I am a self-published writer, or to be more specific I am an indie author. Both of these are writers who have published a book by means other than a traditional publishing house.

A self-published author is one who does it all by him or herself, from the writing, to editing, formatting, and cover design. The indie, or independent author, is the one who bears the cost of publishing, and hires professionals to transform their book into a finished product...

While she was reading, I was transported back in time to those days; the days of banishment and solitude, the days of struggle, and the days of waiting for magazines to publish my short stories even without payment. Then there were the days of the slap in the face that a rejection from an editor was, the days of agent's rejections, and the days of envying famous writers who had made it big. Those were days of painful longing for a publishing contract.

When Suzan had finished reading, all three of them asked, "Was that you?"

"Yes, I was an indie author," I said, "What is the name of the magazine?

"*Sky of Knowledge*," Farah answered.

"Almost sixty years ago, I sent this article," I said with a smile.

"I am proud of you grandpa," Suzan said, "but where are the books that you composed?"

"Unlike nowadays, writing was a life draining task. One must have a mighty good reason to stick to it as a profession. It takes enormous amounts of motivation to keep writing day after day for many years before you get to see any of your products on a shelf. I remember my first book, I wrote nine drafts and spent seven years on it before I could publish it."

Without waiting for them to ask about the book I published, I got up and walked over to the shelf containing my personal journals and notebooks. Pulling a nine by six, dog-eared, yellow paged, paperback novel out, I sniffed the pages, filling every cell in my old brain. My head was swimming and as I turned to face them, Suzan, Lisa and Farah bounced toward me, snatching the novel from my hand they were so excited. I went back to relax on my leather seat.

"Was this your first book grandpa?" Lisa asked.

"The first and the last."

"So what happened, why did you quit?" Suzan asked.

"I did everything I could to find a traditional publisher, as you read in the article. But I got tired of waiting and decided to publish it myself. I hired professionals to design my cover and format my book, then I hired professional editors and in no time the book was published, and I started promoting it. I gave a few readings, and sometimes if I was lucky, three or four people would show up. There were times when I was reading to silent rows of books in the bookshops. I built good relationships with the bookstore managers in the hopes of convincing them to buy my book, but unfortunately, the bookshops by then were all big chains. The decisions for purchasing came from the head office, based on the popularity of the book and the writer. Some managers promised to take a few copies if a client asked for my book, but no one ever asked."

"Oh, Grandpa, that must have been so frustrating," Suzan said. I could see the pitying looks in their eyes.

"Nowadays, composing is so much easier," Lisa said.

"If I had been in your place, I would have given up a lot sooner than you did," Farah said.

"That's not what made me give up."

The three of them remained attentive while I continued spilling my guts while avoiding their eyes. It was just too painful. "I decided to put my book on the shelf in one of the stores where I knew the manager,

4: *The Writer*

without informing her. I figured a client would choose it and the manager would see that my book was in demand. Going to the murder mystery section, I slipped my novel between the books of some of the most famous writers of that genre at that time. Then I went back to the end of the aisle carrying a random book, pretending I was reading, and allowed my eyes to stray from time to time to where I'd put my novel. I spent three painful hours that day, but no one even glanced at my book. So I took my book and left.

I came back the next day, but this time I brought my laptop, so I could write while I waited for someone to pick up my book. I sat on the floor, leaning on the bookshelf at the end of the aisle. I put in a good five hours of writing until my butt was numb from the hard floor, but no one picked up my book. I took my laptop and my book and left. The manager didn't notice me, or at least pretended she didn't see me, and that was ok with me.

The third day I came again with my laptop and started writing after I put my book on the shelf. I didn't put it between the books this time. No, this time I placed it facing the people wandering between the shelves, picking this one and that one. The third day I got lucky and didn't need to wait for five hours. Before the first hour was up, an old man wearing a striped suit and a round hat with a cream silk ribbon, a gray beard, and glasses came in. I thought he was maybe a professor of some kind. He looked like a gentleman to me.

To my surprise, he picked up my book without even reading the book's description; maybe he liked the cover design. He opened his leather hand bag and placed it carefully inside. He moved slowly around the store, looking at other books. I followed him with my eyes and shut down my laptop expectantly when he moved to the next aisle. I pretended to be reading a book cover whenever he looked my way. Finally I could wait no longer, so I went up to the checkout and found the manager there. She noticed my wide smile, and we engaged in a short discussion. Of course I didn't mention anything about my book, as I wanted her to be surprised.

Out of the corner of one eye, I continued to follow the progress of the gentleman's hat as he moved from aisle to aisle. Then, without even glancing our way, he headed to the exit and left the shop. The manager noticed the sudden absence of my smile, and the sweat beading on my forehead. She asked if I needed a glass of water, and I said, "Yes, please."

The Cure

Mekaiel held the book with both hands, squinting at the design on the cover, as if he was absorbing it pixel by pixel. As the founder of the University of Life here in Shanghai, he has influenced plenty of people to change their perspective towards life. When I first saw him, he struck me only as a wealthy man. However, after seeing him day after day, I soon realized how rich he really is spiritually. He is in his sixties, with a benevolent air and graying hair. His face is always clean shaven, no matter what time of day I meet him.

We were in the living room of his apartment on Wulumuqi street in Shanghai. Before I could ask him what he thought about the book cover, he said, more to himself than to me, "Heart breaking." On the cover was a baby, partially buried in the desert with only the bloody feet visible. The title was written in the spilled blood.

"What do you think about the title?" I asked, literally begging him for a compliment. I wasn't sure if he didn't hear my question or he purposely ignored it, because he started to read the description on the back cover, loudly. *'The Victorious Blood portrays a bloody epic which is over thirteen hundred years old. It took place in Karbala, a small town on the bank of the Euphrates river in Iraq. It was between the grandson of the prophet of Islam, al-*

Hussain bin Ali, who commanded an army that did not exceed a hundred warriors. And Yazid bin Mu'awiyah, the son of the founder of the Umayyad state. His army consisted of thirty thousand soldiers under the command of Omar bin Saad.'

Mekaiel's cat Nora came up and rubbed her fluffy body against my leg, meowing for attention. Cat's always seem drawn to me, maybe because they're my favorite animal. So, I picked her up and carried her in the crook of my arm, patting her head automatically while looking around me. Piles of ten kilo sacks of dry cat food, and dozens of boxes filled with cans of wet cat food lined one wall. Even during the coldest winters in Shanghai, Mekaiel hasn't missed a night in ten years, going out with a cart full of cat food to feed stray cats and kittens. He leaves around 11 pm and returns before sunrise. He also keeps a few rescued cats in his apartment.

He finished reading without comment, then raised his eyes to look at me over the top of his glasses. "Why didn't you mention the reason for the battle, Hussin?"

"Well, as you know, many complex reasons for the battle have been discussed over the time since. It would not be possible to mention all of them on the cover; they wouldn't fit." I smiled. "One must read the book to learn the reasons."

He nodded slowly, pushing up his glasses with his pointer finger, "My parents were strong believers in the message of Imam al-Hussain."

"Yes. Just like my parents."

He stopped flipping pages and sat frozen in place, as if time stood still. I looked down at Nora on my lap; she looked back at me with lazy lidded eyes. Finally, he said, "What made you do it? There are thousands of books and research papers about what happened to

4: The Cure

Imam al-Hussain in many languages. Why would you want to add yet another book?"

"On the anniversary of the event each year, the scholars discuss details, but they focus primarily on the religious message, keeping it alive through the generations. Throughout my long years of reading history books, I realized we can learn plenty of lessons that are not only religious. The most astonishing discovery for me was the bravery of the women back then."

"What women? Women were not permitted to fight," he said. "Women during that era were an invisible species who had no influence and no opinion."

"You will be surprised to know that was not completely true," I said. "In the battle of Karbala, Zainab bint Ali played just as big a part as her brother al-Hussain bin Ali, and without the use of either sword or arrow."

"How?"

"I could tell you about it, but if you really want to get the feel of it, you must read the book. The words in the book breath pain and sorrow."

He nodded thoughtfully.

"Plus, it wasn't only Zainab bint Ali who had a powerful role. A number of other women were also known for their contributions to the struggle, and all of them are mentioned in the book."

"I have a brother-in-law who is a Sayyid," Mekaiel said.

The title Sayyid is given to every person considered to be directly descended from the prophet Muhammad through his daughter Fatimah and her husband Imam Ali bin Abi Talib.

"Where does he live?" I asked excitedly.

"He's in Karachi."

"That's amazing, I have not sent a copy of the book to Karachi yet. I bet he knows a lot of young Shia'a who would enjoy and benefit from reading the story."

"This brother-in-law was in a plane crash but miraculously didn't die."

Nora jumped from my arm to the floor as if my astonishment alarmed her, "That would be an interesting story. I'm writing a collection of short stories and your brother-in-law's experiences would make an interesting short story."

"I have tried to convince him of that many times, since my niece is a writer as well. She wanted to write it as a short story, but he simply would not agree. He suffers from depression, just like his father before him and his brother as well."

"I would love to chat with your brother-in-law just to get an understanding of how he is coping with depression at his age."

"You didn't tell me that you have depression."

"I thought I told you a while ago."

"What are you taking for it?'

"SSRI, and Bupropion."

"You don't need medicine to get rid of depression you know?"

"What else is there?"

"I know a cure for depression, without drugs."

I snickered, but when he didn't laugh, I realized he was serious. My cheeks grew hot, as I said, "How does it work?"

Just then, the doorbell rang. Our order from the Qing Zhen restaurant had arrived, so we washed our hands, prepared the table, and sat down to eat our dinner.

While we were enjoying the kabab, Mekaiel said, "Carl Jung very brilliantly postulated many years ago that

4: *The Cure*

all fears, phobias, and mental illnesses are a direct result of mismanagement of our souls. Just like the body, the soul too needs nourishment. Unfortunately, most people live their whole lives without even acknowledging the existence of their soul, let alone expressing gratitude for the sustenance it provides. It's the deprivation of this nourishment which brings about a feeling of emptiness, insecurity, discomfort, depression, and eventually madness. Psychotherapy that does not engage the spiritual aspect of the person involved, is doomed to fail. We cannot do cosmetic surgery on a leaf when the problem lies in the roots of the tree."

"And how is that achieved?" I asked while savoring the tender shank of beef kabab.

"With meditation," he said.

"I thought one of the main purposes of meditation was to accept the situation our body and mind are in and live with it." I couldn't remember where I'd read that, or even if I'd said it correctly.

"There is a huge difference between accepting and living with our circumstances and justifying our actions by claiming we are accepting our circumstances. The sole purpose of the body is to sustain the mind, but the sole purpose of the mind is to navigate our soul closer to God. Period! Amassing a fortune, eating, visiting bathrooms, making babies, preparing pancakes, or even dying are all secondary. You are a spiritual being having a human experience. Our body is temporary, but the soul is permanent."

"I've never meditated, I don't even know how to do it," I said, embarrassed by my confession.

"I can teach you how to meditate. You only need to still your mind and you will be healed from your depression. After a week of meditation you will be the master of your mind and the mind will be still. Then you won't need medicine anymore. That's when you will start being positive and happy."

"I am not taking the medicine to be positive and happy. I was always happy and positive, even before I knew I had depression."

"So, what is the purpose of the medicine then?"

"To reduce the pain of the mind. I think one can suffer pain and still be happy as long as he's positive."

"The soul is trying to convey a message to you and seeking your attention. If you nourish it and give it the required attention, you will gladly give up materialistic pleasure for the pleasure that the soul gives you."

Later, on my way back, I was thinking about what Mekaiel said. I was grateful because when he didn't just tell me not to take medicine; he suggested a replacement. Unlike many other people, who would say you don't need medicine for depression and when you ask them why, their answer is, depression is not a real illness. Sometimes the person who's trying to enlighten my life with this extraordinary discovery, is the same person who needs to go and see a psychologist themselves.

The worst feeling I ever had from depression is that life is meaningless. So I always felt I had to do something to give it meaning and purpose, nothing could instill that feeling in me as much as helping other humans. I figured the best way would be to use what inspired me personally. I have always been influenced by the written word, so I decided to serve other human beings with my words. From that came the persistence I needed to make my dream of becoming a published writer a reality.

So after I published my first novel I realized that not only my life gained meaning and purpose but the

4: *The Cure*

process of writing for others to read helped me ease my depression. So in simple words, I used my depression to achieve my dream, that's why I stopped being reluctant from mentioning that I have depression. In hope of helping someone out who suffers from depression and not having enough courage to fight it. And to convey the message that not only can you defeat depression but also use it to your advantage.

On the Metro

Tell me, what is the weirdest thing you've noticed going on around you? Wait, are you from today's younger generation who have an extra bone in the back of their neck? You know, the ones who can't raise their heads, because they're always bent, looking down at their smartphone screens. If you're one of those, don't bother to continue reading, because you'll never see any of the things I see on a daily basis.

You're not one of those? Ok, great, good to hear, but I still warn you, if you continue to read, it will be at your own risk.

Sigh.

I am Zhologt. No, not Zoloft. My name is Zhologt.

I was on my way to the health center earlier today. No, I didn't have an appointment. As long as I get there before four pm, I can still take a number, register at reception, and wait for my turn.

The few hundred meters from my apartment to the metro station, are like a concentration camp in Siberia during winter. Do they have other seasons than winter in Siberia? The freezing air seeped through my clothes and chilled me to the bone. Down in the metro station, passengers have to wait in queues for the metro to come to a complete stop. I was the first in my queue with two minutes left before the metro would arrive. I knew it would be a race to grab the few empty seats. What do you expect in Shanghai? It has twenty-eight million inhabitants. I knew I'd be lucky if I could find an empty seat at that time of the day.

Usually the people in the queues wait for the arriving passengers to exit the train before they try to enter. But this time when the metro arrived, the queue I was in surged forward, forcing me ahead of them before the arriving passengers could exit. I was forced to push and shove my way onboard, then run looking for an empty seat.

Crap, just as I expected people who entered through other doors had already grabbed all the empty seats. No, there was still one left but as I ran toward it, a bald man appeared out of nowhere and sat down. I looked around like a panicked mother who has lost her kids, but there were no more empty seats, and the car was full. I looked at the bald guy with my lips pressed tightly together. If looks could burn, he would have turned to ashes on the spot. He smiled a sly smile and then ignored me, focusing all of his attention on his smartphone.

The metro lurched forward, and I had to clutch the metal bar to avoid falling backward against the passengers standing near me. The voice on the speaker announced the next station, first in Chinese, then in English. I looked at the bald man. He was still staring at his smartphone's screen just like most of the other passengers. I tried to steal a look at his screen from above, but couldn't quite see it, as he was holding it almost vertical.

On my right was an old lady, on my left, a young man with wireless earphones in his ears. On either side of the bald guy were two women, both playing games on their smartphones. I glanced out the window at the advertisements on the walls of the metro tube. A series of posters showed a young man drinking milk tea, the sequence of the pictures perfectly matched the speed of the train, so it looked like a giant flip movie. Glancing down I noticed the reflection of the bald man's phone in the window behind him. He was swiping through photos and…, oh, crap I broke out in a cold sweat. Was I seeing things? Was that a naked body, or worse, a murdered headless female body?

I was right. The photo he was looking at showed the tiles beneath the body smeared with blood. He swiped again, and the next photo was of the same body, taken from another angle, the woman's private parts were exposed.

I looked cautiously around me. Was I the only one seeing what this man was looking at? No one was even looking in his direction. I focused again on the reflection. Now the photos were from even closer up. The next one was a close up of a bloody neck. I gagged and almost vomited. Closing my eyes tightly, I visualized the bottom of an empty bucket, which is what I think about daily to help me fall asleep. When I opened my eyes again, the reflection on the glass showed he was looking at a photo taken from the side of the body.

What if these are just photos from off the net? What if this guy was some kind of expert? A forensic pathologist, maybe? How silly I am, I thought, but those pictures were disturbing. I kept staring at the reflection in the glass. I was beginning to enjoy spying on him; thinking maybe he was a crime photographer. I continued to watch casually until one photo disturbed me big time.

4: *On the Metro*

The photo made my head swim dizzily. I swallowed hard; my mouth was watering so much. I swallowed again, starting to feel woozy.

Just then the speaker announced my station, and the metro rolled to a stop. Standing outside the train, I continued to watch the bald man through the window, but he didn't notice me. The glass doors closed, and the train started moving away. I kept staring after it until the tail end was swallowed by the darkness of the tube. A security guard was watching me suspiciously.

My cheeks flushed hot as I ran toward the stairs, still seeing the image of the woman's severed head hanging by the hair from the bald man's hand. He had taken a selfie with it. How disgusting. The smile on his face was sickening. I grabbed the handrail to keep from falling down the stairs as I was beginning to feel lightheaded.

Then I glanced at my watch. Wow, three thirty already. I needed to hurry to my appointment so I could get my prescription and buy more medicine. It had to be today. The last thing I wanted was for people to see me entering the mental health clinic two days in a row.

They might think I'm a psycho or something.

Acknowledgements

I would like to thank you for reading my stories. I hope you enjoyed them.

I would like to thank Ryan Thorpe and his writing workshop in Shanghai, where the idea for this book was born. I would also like to thank my editor, William Gould, for his dedication in editing these stories.

Most importantly, I want to thank God for blessing me always and surrounding me with fantastic and supportive family and friends.

I am an indie author, so your reviews would be a great help and support to me. I would be grateful if you review the book on any of the social media platforms and refer the book to your friends, if you like it. Once again, thank you very much for reading.

Hussin Alkheder was born in Damascus, Syria. He lived and grew up in the narrow alleys of Old Damascus. In his first novel, a murder mystery called ***The Daughter of Patience***, he showed us the environment he grew up in, between Damascus and Dubai. His second book, a work of nonfiction, ***The Victorious Blood***, travels back in time 1300 years to portray one of the bloodiest eras in the history of Islam. However, in the ***Four Ladies***, wants to bond with his readers through a collection of short stories influenced by the four cities he's lived in.

Printed in Great Britain
by Amazon